...THE DARK ONE FALLS

THE DARK WAR SAGA BOOK 2

By Michael D. Nadeau

…The Dark One Falls is a work of fiction. Names, characters, places, and incidents are the product of the author's imagination or used fictitiously. Any resemblance to actual persons or faeries—living, dead, or brought back to life with magical artifacts—events, or locales is coincidental. Actions, thoughts, and statements by characters do not express the desires of the author.

…The Dark One Falls

First paperback edition, November 2025, Michael D. Nadeau

Cover art by Daniel Eskridge- shutter stock
Typography and Interior Design by Michael D. Nadeau
Editing by Curtis Alan Provance

ISBN (paperback) 978-1-960654-06-9
ISBN (E-book) 978-1-960654-07-6

Also from
Michael D. Nadeau

The Land of Lythinall Series
The Darkness Returns
The Darkness Within
Tales From Lythinall
The Darkness Falls
The Curse of Seltemver: Tales from Lythinall: Book 2

Rise of the Archmage Series
Dragon Caller
Dragon Master

Angels Among Us

The Dark War Saga
When the light returns…

ACKNOWLEDGMENTS

I would like to thank my wife and friends for inspiring me in my writing, as well as our games that have given this tale life. Thank you to Curtis P. as well for help with editing, and Alan P. for proofing.

MAP OF ALIAN'TIR

CONTENTS

Chapter One: Gathering Darkness	7
Chapter Two: The Steps of Faith	20
Chapter Three: Close to Home	34
Chapter Four: The Hammer Falls	48
Chapter Five: Sacrifices Made	60
Chapter Six: Heroes Fall	73
Chapter Seven: Dark Days	91
Chapter Eight: Decisions Made	105
Chapter Nine: It's Always Darkest…	120
Chapter Ten: …Before the Dawn	140
Epilogue: Just Getting Started	164
Appendix: Glossary	173

CHAPTER ONE — GATHERING DARKNESS

Endless Wastes, North of the Forest of Dust

She trudged through the sand, her shadowy armor affording no help with the soft, dry terrain. Her heavy steps sank deep, and she kept stumbling despite her preternatural strength. Then there was the sand itself. Even though she was undead, she could still feel this cursed stuff getting everywhere; it shouldn't matter, but it increased her irritation at the situation. Callen Drah stopped and stared at the sky, remembering what this desolate landscape used to be, where she grew up, and learned the way of the knight.

The Endless Wastes used to be a verdant forestland called Jal'rien. This beautiful land was home to humans and elves alike, as well as the first documented half-elves in Alian'tir. When the war between Branthian and Tsir'illia erupted, Jal'rien tried to stay neutral but was dragged into the conflict by their council of greedy nobles. Callen was a knight of Jal'rien, often referred to as Dragonknights. They were an elite force of knights that rode sleek elven horses through the forests and fought with deadly skill and grace. The Dragonknights were lured into serving Raer'dreth during the war, which left Jal'rien with only a minimal force, requiring them to lean heavily on Branthian for reinforcements.

In a brilliant strategic move, the elves lured the human knights into northern Jal'rien for a final battle, and Raer'dreth—then just a simple elven archmage—called down dark storms of ruin to smite their knights. His newly crowned Knights of Shad'ar rode behind the storm and slaughtered the remaining defenders in the cities that tried to fight back. Unknown to the elven archmages—and, Callen suspected, even Raer'dreth himself—was the extent of Raer'dreth's shadow magic and what cost it would have. Not only did it slay the human knights and their steeds, but the very forest around them started to wither away. The shadow magic seeped into the ground, rotting the roots of all the trees and plants, and killing every living thing it touched. Even when the war was over, all of Jal'rien withered as the shadows destroyed all who lived there. Those who fled survived, but the shadow taint spread for miles, and not many escaped its touch. As it finally stopped spreading, clear borders were set up by Branthian, and a watch was set, yet the damage could not be fixed.

Within a decade, the forests and lush grass were all turned to sand, and the buildings were swallowed by storms and buried. Today, the only ruins left are of Anor, the former capital of ancient Jal'rien, and a small oasis where the city of G'lar once stood. This city was where the main temple to Amara stood, and rumor has it that the massive lake was saved by the touch of the nature goddess herself; why she didn't save the entire land is anybody's guess.

Stopping at a low dune, Callen Drah looked out at the small horde shuffling towards her and sighed with a breath she didn't need. As a Knight of Shad'ar, she was almost invincible to most mortals in combat. She was centuries old—even if the body she was inhabiting wasn't—and her knowledge and skill were far better than the most skilled warrior humanity could hope to send against her. She *seemed* human, with her dark, shadowed armor flowing around her like smoke and long copper hair spilling out from her helm upon broad shoulders; the resemblance ended there, however. Twin pools of liquid fire burned within that black helm, and her voice sounded like the whispers of the grave.

I haven't been here since that day, Callen thought as the horde shuffled closer. *It doesn't even feel like home.* She shook her head to clear it and set her shoulders. Living in the past was what got the nobles of Jal'rien killed, and she learned a valuable lesson that day: when you give in to greed and live for power, people die.

The shuffling dead stopped near her and looked around aimlessly, awaiting her command. They were all barely skeletons, wearing tattered clothes and carrying rusted weapons with sand still spilling out of their empty eye sockets and open mouths. Callen could discern which were Jal'riens and which weren't by their weapons. The scimitars—curved swords meant for agile warriors—were what the militia of Jal'rien used, and the others were probably ancient Branthians or even elves.

"All right, let's go," she said out loud to the gathered horde before her. Her master, Raer'dreth, had lent her this force to destroy the southern Lorant cities and slay the upstart heroes that almost killed her...again. Just thinking about that infuriating dwarf made her shake with barely constrained rage, igniting her shadowblade without meaning to. The black flames danced upon the blade as ash slowly dripped onto the sand. "And that infernal sword!" she cursed loudly to know one in particular. She was venting now, a very human thing to do for someone who hadn't been truly alive for a very long time.

It had been over a tenday since the sword Dar'kir had almost killed her again, slicing through her armor like it was mist instead of enchanted, hardened leather. She knew of the sword from ages past and was there when Hardin Lor slew the elven wizard wielding it. She should've recognized it when she first saw the man in black, but she was a little busy trying to kill that thrice-damned dwarf. Callen Drah turned and marched back toward the Forest of Dust with her horde following and almost missed the pair of dwarves spying on her; the audible gasp of surprise drew her horrific gaze, and she smiled inside her helm.

Danni and Lanni Hoarfren were out playing deep in the Forest of Dust, where they were not supposed to be. They were, in fact, always where they weren't supposed to be; it was part of their charm. They were dwarven twins—even rarer than elven twins—and had only seen twelve summers. They were both brown-haired and dark-eyed, each only standing about three and a half feet tall. Danni had the beginnings of a beard, and his sister only had slight fuzz, which was something they fought over constantly. It was actually what they were shouting about at this very moment.

"Why do ye get to lead the way?" Lanni asked as they circled a tall tree.

"Because I'm the one with tha beard," Danni replied smugly. He stroked his wisps of hair and beamed proudly, almost tripping over a high root.

"Well, beard or not, you're horrible at leading," Lanni said, sticking out her tongue. "Besides, I have mine coming in right now, too."

"That thing? It's like the fur of a gnarr's leg, for Gar'heth's sake." Danni ducked as his sister threw a branch at him. "You know what? Fine, you lead the way," he said, throwing his stick at his sister.

Lanni walked by and shouldered her brother playfully. "I think I will." Lanni led them over a rise and into the north. She knew this from the sun in the sky—something her father taught her last year while Danni was busy learning how to properly smith on a cold anvil. They took turns at their craft so as not to compete too much; little did their parents know that they competed at everything else to make up for it. As they walked over the rise, they could both see figures out in the wastelands. The Endless Wastes were off limits, and it was the one place they both agreed not to go.

"Who is that?" Danni asked, crouching down low.

"I'm not sure, but they shouldn't be out there." Lanni had a bad feeling in her gut—something else her father had taught her to always listen to. "We should leave."

"Hold on, we have to see who it is so we can tell someone," Danni said, getting down on his stomach and crawling forward.

"Wait," Lanni started to say, then shrugged with a frown. She couldn't let her twin go all alone. Crawling on her stomach, Lanni caught up to her brother, and they both got to the edge of the forest, hiding behind a clump of dead ferns. "If we're quiet, they won't see us," she said, but a second later, both young children gasped loudly as what they were seeing came fully into view...the dead walking of their own accord.

"Gods!" Danni swore, leaping to his feet. "Lanni, run!"

Lanni was frozen with a dread she had never felt before. The skeletons of the dead were walking and holding weapons, just like those scary tales she had heard; these, though, were nothing like the stories. The dead were shuffling with missing bones, with some of them missing parts of their face and jaw, sand still slowly spilling out of their eyes and mouth. Tattered clothes were ripped and stained, swaying in the breeze...a breeze that also brought their wicked smell.

Worse than that was the dark knight that now strode towards them both. The figure was dressed in shadowy armor and had blazing fire for eyes, eyes that were staring straight at them both! This was no shuffling dead, but a cold warrior of death. A hard, stinging sensation in her face snapped Lanni out of the gripping fear.

"Run!" Danni said as he slapped Lanni again in the face. "Run now!" he called, dragging Lanni by the arm.

Lanni was crying now, her tears barely falling before they were swept away by the rushing wind as she fled. They were a long way from their village—almost a full day's run—and even though dwarves barely tired, she didn't think they could outrun what was coming. She risked a look back and saw the knight raise a black sword that leaked shadows and swing it at them.

Danni must have seen it, too, because he shouldered his sister into a bush as the dark magic neared. "Run, Lanni, and know that I love ya', Sis!"

Lanni rolled and came to her knees, looking at her twin as the black shadows hit him. Ash formed around his arms, burning him instantly as some of it snaked its way into his screaming mouth. His frantic gurgles and thrashing were enough to send terror racing through Lanni's soul as she got to her feet and ran. "I'm sorry, Danni!" she cried as she pumped her legs as hard as she could. Lanni was dodging now through the trees so as not to get hit by whatever magic that dark knight had thrown at them. *Fifty miles you have to run, girl,* she thought to herself, trying to control her breathing as she sobbed, but it was hard.

The image of her brother screaming and dying lent her strength, though, and she sniffed back her tears and clenched her teeth. *What was it Mother always said? It's hard to cry when you're angry.* Lanni ignored that empty hole in her chest where her twin used to be and concentrated on how angry she was that he died; died because he had saved her. "I'll see you dead for this!" she wailed to the forest around her as branches scratched her face and tore her clothes. She was running heedless of them all right now, just focusing on getting away. *You can do this, girl, for Danni.*

South Bridge, Southern Branthian

The young man watched the sun set slowly in the distance as his horse trotted across the plains of Branthian, the coming evening painting reds and golds across the beautiful sky. This nation was his home, and he knew that, with the coming war, he had to enjoy these moments whilst he could. Alant Landsir sighed as he turned his gaze toward the Endless Wastes in the East. He knew that the soldiers and knights of Branthian fought—and died—even now against legions of undead that were shambling out of the sands, awoken by foul magic. He had seen these skeletons himself, fighting alongside the Knights of the Realm. It was what had earned him the respect of the knights; wielding a legendary sword didn't hurt either.

Alant—or Silverlord Landsir as the king had dubbed him—was young for the weight he now carried, though you couldn't tell from the size of the young man. At only sixteen summers, Alant was over six feet and weighed fifteen stone.

Unlike most nobles with haughty titles, Alant had earned the title bestowed upon him twice over. He had slain a powerful evil and saved countless lives, uniting the nations of Tsir'illia and Branthian against the dark forces coming for all of them. The young squire had saved the Knight-Captain of the Knights of the Realm against the undead coming out of the Endless Wastes and was now wielding not one, but two ancient armaments of power. Alant brushed his black hair out of his cinnamon eyes and smiled despite the harrowing events of the last two tendays. That smile was reserved for his love, who rode in front of him, the tiny faerie warrior currently sitting on his lap.

"Giddy up!" Syn'ella called out to the animal as she snapped the reins playfully. The faerie was bouncing with the reins in her tiny hand; her wings folded neatly behind her. "I never knew this was so much fun, Alant," she said, looking up over her shoulder at him. Syn'ella was one of the faerie folk who lived in Tsir'illia and met Alant when this all started. Syn'ella had long golden hair and deep golden eyes, with gossamer wings that usually spread out behind her. She was only two and a half feet tall and weighed no more than one stone, yet her beauty was unmistakable with her smooth, pale skin and all the curves of a real woman.

"Hold for a moment, brave Syn'ella," Alant said, taking the reins and stopping the horse. He pointed ahead of them as a column of refugees came in front of knights on horseback. "There are more survivors from Saer'lan."

Syn'ella flew up and squinted into the fading light. "Hey, I see them. Thank Amara that the Knight-Captain rode there first," she said as she made the sign of the nature goddess. Most elves and faeries, as well as most sorcerers, worshipped Amara—Goddess of Magic and Nature.

"Yes. I'm glad he chose that path. That is the third group of refugees out of the city now, and it should be the last." Alant had stopped the horse in case they needed help, but he could see that they weren't being pursued. The young Silverlord handed the reins back to Syn'ella with a kiss on her head, and they resumed their course toward the southern bridge. He didn't want to get caught up in questions from the knights if he could avoid it; he hated explaining his new title to those in the field who might have scoffed at the news.

"Do you think we'll see more of the dead in the south?" Syn'ella asked as they rode.

"I'm almost sure of it. If Raer'dreth is an ancient archmage, then he won't be stupid," Alant said, frowning now. *To think that all the scary stories about that guy were true,* he thought. "I wouldn't think he would send all his forces in one direction or all at the same time; so, they must be leaving the wastes from all directions, even after all this time since they started; no doubt we'll see more fighting on the way to Lorant."

"I'm so excited for this trip," Syn'ella said. "I've only heard about Lorant and have *never* met a dwarf before."

Alant laughed at her excitement, reveling in the spirit of the tiny warrior. He, too, had never been to that nation and was looking forward to seeing what awaited them. Lorant was the easternmost nation on the continent of Alian'tir and was home to dwarves as well as humans. While there were rumors of some dwarves coming into the far south of Branthian, they only numbered in the dozens, if that, and it had been in the last tenday or so. Where Alant and Syn'ella were headed, dwarves would be a common sight. "I've only read about them in stories," Alant admitted. "Though the histories have some horrible things to say about the war they had with Lorant."

"Well, you can't always trust stories. Look at us." Syn'ella said, leaning back into his arms as they rode. "You should hear some of the tales about humans that faeries tell to their children at bedtime. You're not at all that violent or ugly."

"Fair point, my love." Alant stopped as he saw another column of knights at the bridge. To his knowledge, there were no regiments heading south to reinforce Fort Yarin; the Knight-Captain of the south had sent word that they were holding steady with minimal contact. *So, what are those knights doing?* he thought as he tried to get a better look at them. The closer they got, his stomach dropped. These knights weren't marching in any sort of order, nor were they in line; they were shambling along like the dead!

Just as he realized this, Syn'ella saw the awful truth as well. "Alant...those knights are dead!"

"I see it too, Syn'ella, hold on. We have to get by these things and warn the people of Folris." Alant took the reins from her and kicked the horse into a gallop, trying to keep to the far side of the bridge. The knights turned their vacant eyes toward him as he guided the horse by, and his heart broke when he indeed recognized a few of the men. These were the fallen knights from the skirmish of Calian with whom he had fought. That battle was only won by brave Syn'ella's accomplishment of bringing reinforcements, but they had still lost men. Those knights were buried with honor where they fell, for haste was needed to get word to the king; Knight-Captain Marveth hated leaving them, but his duty was clear.

Now, however, it seemed that the foul magic that had brought forth the ancient dead was also reanimating anything that had died near the sands. The dead shuffled on as Alant rode by; their relentless march never hesitating, despite their wounds. The knights were still dressed in armor—slashed and rent by the enemy that had slain them—and their withered flesh gripped their swords loosely. The milky, glazed look of their eyes was horrible, as was the rotting flesh falling off here and there as they walked. It had been almost two tendays, and already the ground had ravaged their bodies in an attempt to reclaim them into itself.

They left the dead behind, galloping hard now to warn the people of Folris.

"There! I see the village," Syn'ella exclaimed in a couple of minutes as their horse galloped over the plains.

Alant frowned and prayed to Zomnus—God of Luck and Fate—that the local guard had heard of his title; they didn't have time to rehash the entire story again. Even though King Danrae had sent out an official announcement, some knights claimed ignorance and refused to listen to him. Syn'ella set them straight, of course, and most knights had heard how she had bested Knight-Commander Feskar in battle. The sound of children playing snapped Alant out of his reflection, and he took stock of the village before him as they slowed.

Folris was a small fishing village just north of Fort Yarin. Officially, they were told to evacuate with the rest of the towns in Branthian. However, the Lord of Oliar—a city to the west of Folris—had waved a dismissive hand and sent a messenger, letting the king know that the southern region was free of the dead and that Fort Yarin was more than capable of defending them. King Danrae was furious, but short of stripping the man of his title and sending men to evacuate himself, there was nothing to be done; Branthian didn't have the manpower to do that at the moment. The king did send back his own missive, however, stating that when this was over, the Lordship would be looked at with closer study.

"We have company, Alant," Syn'ella warned as she pointed to an armed guard approaching on horseback. The sun had set, but the twilight was still enough to see the men riding toward them.

The local guard, dressed in hardened leather armor and shields, rode with the Branthian standard flying high. They rode with weapons drawn and slowed when they approached, their leader moving his horse forward. "I am Lieutenant Oron Haves, of the Branthian guard. State your name and reason for traveling to Folris," the soldier commanded. The man had to be at least thirty summers and was well-built. He had close-cropped brown hair and dark eyes, along with a scar that ran down the entire right side of his face.

Alant was pleased they were taking travelers so seriously, at least, yet an undercurrent of worry still gnawed at him. "I am Silverlord Landsir, and I travel by the leave of King Danrae."

"Ah, Silverlord. We of the southern regions have heard of your promotion and the grave tidings of war. What can we do to assist you? My scouts told me of a horse approaching at speed, and I was worried." The lieutenant smiled warmly and waved to his men to stand down. The soldiers all visibly relaxed.

"Well, Lieutenant, I hate to ruin your good mood, but you have a problem coming across the bridge, and they should be here by full dark," Alant started, dismounting and leading his horse as they went back into the village proper. He noticed the other soldiers staring at Syn'ella as she let her wings out and flew around to stretch.

"What's coming?" Haves asked with dread. "Is the King sending an armed force to deal with Oliar?"

"No, not as yet," Alant replied, sensing now that this was the reason for the armed greeting. *Maybe the Lord of Oliar is thinking of seceding?* Alant thought, and he shook his head. "This problem is much worse than politics. The risen dead are walking toward your village, yet only nine or so," Alant said as he looked around the small village. He could see children playing and skipping around, and it made his heart tremble at the thought of what the dead would do here if he hadn't come through. "If we set up on the edge of the village with all your men, we should be able to take them out easily and without casualties."

"Yet you stated there were only nine of them." Haves said with a wry smile. "Surely I can send a small group..."

"The dead fight differently than the living, Lieutenant. Those nine men are fallen knights of Branthian and are dressed in armor. It will take every man we have to take them out."

A woman walking towards them had heard Alant's dire warnings and started running towards the road, dropping her basket. "My children are out there!"

"Wait!" Syn'ella cried out, catching the woman and holding her back. "We saw no children on the way into the village. What do you mean?"

"Jess and Madra are shy and hide when people get close. They often play by the thick bushes about a half mile from the bridge and pick berries." The woman was crying now, fighting to get the faerie to let go.

"Stop!" Alant said in the deepest voice he could muster. The woman looked at him with wonder and a little fear, then he softened his smile and leapt on his horse. "I will get the children. Syn'ella, get the soldiers to set up barricades and get ready. I'm not fighting them all, but I may be able to take a couple out to make it easier for them."

The faerie warrior opened her mouth to argue, but closed it and nodded. They shared a bond now, and he knew she could feel his resolve; there was no stopping him. "Take care, my love."

"You're not going alone—Silverlord or not," Lieutenant Haves said as he mounted up and drew his sword once more. Another soldier handed the lieutenant a torch as the sun had set further, and another man handed one to Alant.

"Then let us ride," Alant said as he strapped the Banner of Branthian on his arm and took the brand. The shield hummed as he kicked his horse back around.

CHAPTER TWO — THE STEPS OF FATE

Village of Ilren, Northern Tsir'illia

He walked out of the forest towards the town of Ilren and couldn't help but smile—if you could call what he did now a smile. His head was nothing but a bare skull, with flickering green flames for eyes. The body he was in was likewise almost completely bones, but he wore a rent set of plate over it for now. His bone hands gripped a huge hammer, inlaid with runes and elven symbols, and he was carrying a dented shield. Samor Cah was a Knight of Shad'ar, and as such was immortal, yet something had gone horribly wrong.

He remembered dying—killed by that young whelp of a knight with the sword Ilen'dar. Samor knew that name from long, long ago—the sword used against his fellow knights during the Wasting War. He should've recognized it, but he had been too busy slaughtering the people of Branthian to notice. The dark knight's death felt different this time, almost final. *I know I never made it to my soulgem this time, so how did Raer'dreth bring me back?* he wondered for the hundredth time since crawling out of the cold ground. He knew his master had called him back into the remains of a long-dead warrior; yet, what went wrong? They had all heard the tales of what could go wrong—it was something he and his fellow knights often discussed back when they signed their pact with the dark elven archmage—but he had never thought to experience it himself. *Am I even still considered a Knight of Shad'ar?* Samor shook his skull and snapped out of his dark thoughts, looking once again at the village before him. He needed something to focus on instead of his own fate, and killing was just the remedy.

The village of Ilren was a quaint little elven community, complete with a wizard tower and fields of growing crops. Elven children danced and played while the women and men of the village went about their day. The guards seemed lax and talked amongst themselves instead of keeping their eyes on the tree line, else they would've seen their doom standing there. To the north and west, great fields of wheat grew among rolling hills, and a statue stood tall and proud of some warrior with a sword. Unlike his last slaughter, Samor did not have his shadowblade to throw ash and death at his enemies. This time, he would have only his age-old skill and his preternatural strength; it would suffice. He strode out and across the fields, his heavy footfalls sinking into the earth despite only being bone. Shouts of alarm finally went up when children screamed at the sight of the dark knight, and guards rushed out to meet him with spear and sword.

"Back, creature of darkness," one elven woman said, her sword steady in her delicate hands. "Who are you to walk these lands?"

Samor assumed he no longer had the prophecy surrounding him, but it mattered not. What he *did* still have, however, was his honor, instilled in him back when he first became a knight. In fact, he had more control now than he had all these years; the compulsion to slay was his own, finally. He remembered his old code as if it were yesterday, even though the realm of Jal'rien was nothing but dust these past centuries.

"I am Samor Cah, former Knight of Shad'ar and your doom on this day." *Always give your name when asked; your enemies must know who defeats them,* Samor thought as the first elf leapt high and came down with a spear aimed at his heart. He threw his shield in place and bent his knees, taking the hit like it was nothing, then smashing the elf aside with his hammer. The elf rolled and got to his knees slowly, winded by the powerful blow.

Another elf spun in with a shield and sword, slashing at the knight's skull while sidestepping. This one looked at his kneeling comrade and frowned. "Go, Trin'al, get the children out and gain your breath."

"Yes, elf, gather those that cannot fight and usher them out of my path so that the rest of you can fall to me," Samor said to Trin'al. *Always fight with honor and respect; let your enemies know that you are the better person.* He went over the code as he spun, taking the sword-wielding elf in the chest with the haft of the hammer, then spinning the weapon around and smashing it into his head as he tried to get his shield up. The hammer caved in his skull, crushing half of his head as the body crumpled at his feet. Samor took a step back as the other woman—the one with steady hands on her blade—advanced with murder in her gleaming eyes.

"Monster!" she cried as one hand wove patterns in the air. Flames leapt from her fingertips and engulfed him, burning him from inside his own armor. "I am Captain Ari'kel Everblade, and you will perish for that." More elves came running now, at least two with robes and staves.

Samor felt the fire creep into his armor, seeking his flesh, yet he had none. Still, the flames went through his bones, but only singed them; his animated body took the brunt of the magic as if it were nothing. "I cannot die, dear captain. It is futile to hope for anything but a good death. Bring your worst," Samor announced as he widened his feet and turned slightly sideways, waiting for her predictable charge. *Never surrender when faced with overwhelming odds; let your enemies know that you fear nothing, not even death at their hands.* This last part of his old code made his green flames burn brighter, empowering him deep down somehow. As he saw the elf come in with a timed charge and thrust, Samor spun, coming around with his shield to bash her in the back and send her reeling just as ice formed around his feet. He looked down and bashed the ice with the hammer, freeing himself as the woman stood.

"You stand no chance, creature of darkness," an elf with a gold robe said as his hands spun in intricate patterns.

Samor felt something gather inside of him, a power he had never felt. When he was under the command of Raer'dreth, he had barely any control over what he could or couldn't do; only his honor could give him respite from that magical chokehold. Now, however, there was a power there left untapped. He turned his gaze upon the elf that was casting and felt it shoot up his torso to his skull. Green fire lashed out and consumed the wizard, the elf's wailing screams echoing across the fields as the green flame tore into his flesh like a ravenous beast. The elf fell to ash as the flames left a charred mark on the grass

"Go," Captain Everblade called to the others as she stood bravely in front of Samor. "Get as many away as you can and flee. I will hold this monster here."

Samor nodded to her and stepped in, bashing her with his shield. As she sidestepped and slashed his shield arm, he came down with his skull and slammed her in the head. The dark knight followed it up with a hammer to the chest, then another shield bash, dropping her to her back on the grass. His foot came down on her stomach, cracking the lower ribs with ease as she gritted her teeth to keep from screaming.

"*Ari'kel*!" a younger wizard called out, sending a ray of brilliant blue light at Samor.

Samor caught the beam on the shield, yet the magic disintegrated the ancient metal as well as his armor around that arm. Staggering back, Samor brought his gaze around once again and shot green fire at the young wizard, his anger making the flames more intense. The elf's robes went up in an unholy fire, burning the elf to ash before he could even scream this time. Samor saw that the other guards were fleeing now, women and children crying before them as they jumped on horseback and piled into carts.

"Why is it always carts?" Samor asked Ari'kel as he looked down at her. "I swear you people keep them just to get away." He reached down and grabbed her hair in a bone fist and dragged her into the village. "Now, you are going to watch me tear this entire village down and set it to flame..." Samor began, yet the elven captain kicked out and twisted in his grip, trying to get away. Samor lifted her by the hair higher—ripping half of it out of her head as he did so—and slammed her back down into the dirt. Her whimpering cry let him know the fight had finally left the feisty warrior. "Much better. Now, as I was saying. After you watch me raze this place, you are going to deliver a message to your queen."

Ari'kel lifted her bleeding head and spit at him before falling back down and crying softly. "I will do no such thing."

"You *will* do this unless you want all the villages to suffer this same fate," Samor said. "Choose wisely."

"What is your damned message, foul creature?"

"Tell your queen that I will await her in battle in the fields to the northwest of here. There she will face her doom." Samor kicked Ari'kel squarely in the face, knocking her unconscious. He replaced his ancient, damaged armor with a set from one of the elves, the dark chain and plate suiting him nicely. He also took a shield off a body and fitted it on, testing the weight. *These elves and their light metal,* he thought as he marveled at how little it weighed. He even found a steed decked out in armor—more than likely the captain's, since it was a little larger.

Samor cocked his head to one side as a whisper came to him. It was almost like the magic that brought him to life was still there, guiding him; first, it was the flames he could shoot, and now this. The whispers mentioned a piece of his bone and the horse. *Well, what could go wrong?* he wondered. *Maybe a piece of my bone could make this thing loyal to me?* Acting on instinct, Samor snapped off a small bone from his off-hand and jammed it into the neck of the animal. The beast reared up in horror and pain, thrashing and falling over on the ground. The horse gave a strangled cry as blood poured out of its eyes and mouth, and in less than a heartbeat, it was dead. In the span of two more heartbeats, the animal was back up, those eyes glowing with an intense red fire.

"Well, would you look at that," Samor said to the beast as he ran his bony hand down its neck. "I made myself a friend." The dark knight wondered what Raer'dreth would say about this and laughed as he realized he didn't care. He was getting guidance from someone—or something—and gods burn if he was going to ignore them. Samor Cah set about burning the village down to the ground while his new friend ran across the fields, stamping the dead bodies into the dirt.

North of Folris, Southern Branthian

He peered into the coming gloom for any sign, hoping to find the children quickly and without trouble. Alant and Lieutenant Haves hadn't gone far before a growing concern grew in the pit of his stomach that they wouldn't find the two children in the fading light of day. The minutes stretched long in his young mind, but soon they reached what could only be the thick bushes the woman was talking about. Alant saw the dead wading through the bush like they were searching for something and knew they were just in time. Thankfully, they still had a sliver of light left, but it wouldn't last long.

"Gar'heth's blade!" Lieutenant Haves swore as he saw the figures of the knights shambling around. Their hideous features were obscured until they turned to face him.

"Jess! Madra! Come to the light if you can hear me," Alant said, drawing his sword, Ilen'dar. The sword burst free and immediately lit up the area around him like the sun, reacting to his need. The sword never ceased to amaze the young warrior as it seemed to know what he needed at times. He should have spent more time with Hylana going over the sword and what it could do, but he was eager to explore his bond with Syn'ella first; now, he almost regretted that. Almost.

The dead came at the two warriors now, having a tangible foe to attack. Alant dispatched one knight quickly, but another took its place. Alant circled the dead as they came on, swinging Ilen'dar to keep them at bay and searching for the kids.

"Here!" a boy's voice cried out. The boy ran from the bushes toward Lieutenant Haves, dragging his little sister behind him. Both children were tear-streaked and petrified, and rightly so.

Lieutenant Haves spun his horse around and grabbed the boy with a hand, pulling him up into the saddle just as one of the dead swung. The lieutenant took the hit on his arm and cried out as he pulled the girl up as well. As soon as both children were stable, another one of the dead dragged Haves from the horse.

"Lieutenant!" Alant cried out as he leapt off his horse and swung his sword. He took out one of the dead, then another, but they got right back up. The wounds weren't fatal to something already dead, and he had no time to cleanly take them apart; these armored dead were harder to kill than the bone horrors from before. Alant got to Haves' side and stabbed one of the knights in the face with Ilen'dar, its light burning the flesh away and dropping the creature. *Well, that's new*, he thought as he pulled Haves to his feet and blocked a sword with his enchanted shield. He barely felt the impact; such was the strength of the shield.

The Lieutenant spun and slapped his horse with his good arm, crying out for the children to ride home, then lifted his sword. "Fight well and die better," he said to Alant as the dead came on.

"I have a better idea," Alant countered, slashing at two knights and blocking a third. He grabbed Haves and ran through the dead to Alant's horse, which was kicking and braying in fear. "Get on. I'll hold these things off."

Lieutenant Haves calmed the horse easily, then pulled himself up with an agonizing cry of pain, his arm a ruined mess from the attack.

Once Lieutenant Haves was on the horse, Alant swung Ilen'dar in a sweeping arc and vaulted into the saddle, kicking the horse toward Folris and leaving the dead behind. Alant had only dropped three permanently—never to rise again—but it was good enough. "They will be a lot easier with barricades and more warriors," Alant said as they rode.

"They will be a lot easier with you fighting with us," Haves replied. "Thank you, Silverlord, for the rescue."

"Anytime, Lieutenant, you can repay me by telling me the story of that scar tomorrow over an ale."

Capital City of Llor, Nation of Lorant

Alsan Brenshin walked toward the throne room with hurried steps, her brow creased. She could hear her brother mumbling to himself once again; it was happening more and more of late. Her brother, Albron, had inherited the throne and had stopped the war nearly five years ago, but he had been a mess ever since. With the deaths of the nobles and the end of the treaty with Tsir'illia, the young king had spiraled even further. Alsan walked by a floor-length mirror in the outer hall and stopped, admiring herself before confronting her brother yet again this tenday.

Alsan was truly the daughter of the late Alban Brenshin, right down to the rugged jawline and broad shoulders, even if she was a bastard child. She was a little over five feet tall and thin, yet her hips flared out in all the right places. She had long brown hair with two braids on the sides, deep brown eyes, and a full set of lips with a devastating smile. More handsome than beautiful, Alsan could still reel in the men when it suited her—

and it always suited her. She was wearing a gown of yellow silk hemmed with silver and had lace woven into her hair as a covering. Tiny yellow beads adorned her twin braids as they dropped down over her bosom—another extremely attractive asset that she had.

"Are you here to meet with the king as well, my fair lady?" a melodic voice asked from behind her.

Alsan turned with a fake smile, then her mouth hit the floor. She had heard that the elf girl coming to sign the treaty had arrived with her retinue, but Alsan heard they fled south when that dark knight chased them off. Though she had, of course, heard of elves and knew they were real, she had never before beheld one with her own eyes. The elf before her was short—all but five feet tall if he was an inch—and had short white hair and the most calming emerald eyes she had ever seen. He was dressed in white silk with gold trim, and his cape was dark green with a house symbol on the clasp. He held a small rod, adorned with emeralds and moonstone gems on the small head.

"Milady?"

"Forgive my rudeness, Sir elf, I have never before beheld one of your kind in person and I fear the sight has stunned me," Alsan said with grace and a certain amount of healthy flirting.

"Ah, you flatter a humble servant, fair lady," the elf said, bowing low with a dramatic sweep of his arm. "I am but a steward to the Ambassador of Tsir'illia—Ongril Silvertree at your service."

"I see your tongue betrays your humble nature, Sir Ongril. I am Lady Alsan, daughter of the late Alban," she said, curtsying and holding her gown out wide so she showed more leg than was normal. It was that lyrical voice—and those eyes—that made her just want to back him against the wall and take him right here and now.

"I wasn't aware the late king had a daughter," Ongril said with genuine curiosity. He looked her up and down as discreetly as he could, and his eyes seemed pleased with what he saw.

"I am somewhat of a dirty little secret," Alsan said with a sideways smirk, fanning herself as she turned. She could always tell when someone was being disingenuous, and unless this elf was an elven master, he was honestly intrigued. "I was born of an affair with a mystery woman who wanted money instead of a daughter. When she left with her payment, my father raised me quietly as his own and loved me regardless; despite his flaws—and he had many, I assure you—his love for me wasn't one of them."

"You have satiated my thirst for knowledge for this day, fair lady," Ongril said, bowing again and taking her hand. "Your secret will never pass these lips." He kissed her hand softly then and stood with a flare.

Alsan was truly smitten and could hardly think straight. If all elves could do this, she needed to go see Tsir'illia's court immediately. "Are you meeting with the king this day?" she asked, remembering his initial question.

"That remains to be seen. I've been trying for an audience for three days now, and he has yet to have an opening," the elven steward said with a shrug. "I have time, though, so I continue to check daily."

"I am on my way in to see him as we speak, let me nudge him a little," Alsan said with a smile. "Maybe you can make it up to me later?" She drew in a deep breath and watched his eyes drift down to her chest ever so slightly; he was good at controlling his gaze, but not perfect.

"That would be most pleasing to me, my lady," Ongril answered with a slow smile. That smile brightened his eyes and made her knees tremble a little.

Alsan turned and walked away, with a sway in her step that would make him continue to watch her for the rest of the long hallway. She took deep, quiet breaths to calm herself and looked at the guards outside with a well-practiced smile. "I'm expected, boys. Clear the way." Alsan pushed by them with the force of her personality alone and opened the throne room doors, closing them behind her.

"Ah, a visit from my dearest sister; this can't be good," Albron said with more than a little sarcasm. King Albron Brenshin was sulking, and he sat slumped on his throne like a child who had been scolded. He was of average height and had shaggy brown hair that fell into his faded brown eyes. The rich black robe he wore looked like he hadn't taken it off in over a tenday, and his sword lay on the ground next to the throne like a discarded toy.

"Albron, I heard about the deaths of the nobles and the flight of the elven ambassador. What happened?" Alsan asked as she walked cautiously towards the throne. The guards on either side of the throne were standing at attention with their hands on their swords as if they would be attacked any minute; something they never did in all the years she had seen them.

"That was days ago," the king said flatly. "Where have you been?"

Alsan lowered her eyes and took another breath; he wasn't wrong. She had heard but didn't want to believe the rumors at first. The death—nay, murder—of all of the ruling nobles was all anyone could talk about. It placed the king in an untouchable position with no ruling council to watch his actions and suggest options. The lesser nobles were all in hiding, and most of the ranking guard were debating leaving for the south. "I was waiting until the rumors died down and the eyes of the people weren't all over this place," she answered calmly. "You know Father always wanted me in the background."

“Ah, that’s right. Daddy’s little mistake can’t be seen in public with me,” Albron said with a sad laugh.

“Watch it, brother,” Alsan warned, taking a step closer. That action caused the guards to draw steel, and she stopped in shock. “Really, Albron?”

“Dear *Sister*,” Albron spat with a venom she had never heard from him before. “Now is not a good time. My conscience is a little frayed at the moment.”

“Have you truly sided with the dark knight and her master then?” Alsan asked quietly. She didn’t want to believe he had a choice, preferring to think he was forced into it, yet his attitude would suggest that he chose this—chose this fate for all of them. “Have you forsaken the elves to the north?”

“It’s not like I had much of a choice, Alsan,” Albron lamented as he stood. He walked towards her, his eyes taking on a haunted look as he approached. “That *thing* wanted the elf girl and her companions and I did what I thought my nation needed.”

“It killed all of the high nobles, did you know that?”

“Of course, I heard...I gave them to her as part of the deal. Trust me when I say that we had nothing that could’ve stopped her if we wanted to,” Albron said. “She is a Shadowknight.”

The name hit Alsan in the stomach like a dwarven hammer. Her hand went to her chest, and she held her breath. Shadowknights were a nightmare from the old stories and were said to be immortal. If her brother had truly sided with such a monstrosity, then he had turned his back on the light and all of the people of Lorant. “Albron...” she started to say before his upraised hand stalled her.

“No more lectures, Alsan. Go and hide in your room and stay out of it.” Albron turned sharply and stalked back to his throne. “Escort the lady out,” he said to his guard with a tone of finality.

"Don't bother, I know the way," Alsan sneered, turning on her heel and storming off. She couldn't do anything without proof, but something had to be done. Lorant couldn't survive if they sided with anyone who used those nightmares to get their way. She burst out of the throne room and slammed the doors closed behind her. Alsan only took three steps before she was crying and dropped to her knees.

"I've got you, milady," Ongril said as he enfolded his arms around her and lifted her up. "Let us go and sit somewhere so you may rest."

"We can go to my suite," Alsan answered as she wiped her tears away. She knew that they would have privacy there as Albron never went to her rooms. "He gave in to the dark, dear Ongril. I fear my brother is lost to that evil," Alsan said, composing herself once more.

"I saw firsthand what that dark knight can do, milady," the elf said as they walked. "I fear it may be worse than you think." After they left the grand hall, Alsan stood on her own, her back straight once more despite the tear streaks down her face. "You are here to convince my brother to rethink his allegiance, aren't you?"

"I have to try," Ongril said sadly.

"It's true then? Everyone at Fort Alreth is dead?"

"I'm afraid so, Milady."

"Let us go somewhere private, and you can tell me all about your journey and the horrors you've seen. My brother won't hear you, but maybe both of us can find a way to save our people."

"I would be honored, great lady," Ongril said. "Should I summon the rest of the retinue?"

"I think the talk we may have could turn...personal," Alsan said as she led him up the stairs. She needed time to clear her head, and she knew just the thing to do it.

CHAPTER THREE — CLOSE TO HOME

Northern Tsir'illia, The Queen's Tower

She paced back and forth near the huge window overlooking the forest, barely able to keep her small hands still behind her back. Queen Tolandra had received news of the badly wounded messenger and had the handmaiden rush to bring the woman directly to her chambers after being healed enough to speak. The Queen didn't want any rumors running through the tower until she heard the news first; she knew how servants talked. Tolandra Asil was immaculately beautiful, with long white hair, large gossamer wings, and deep sapphire eyes. She was of mixed elven and faerie descent and had ruled over the nation of Tsir'illia for well over one hundred years.

Tolandra had heard of the destruction of Illren and had tried to use her spells to discern the cause, but something had blocked her magic; that was something that had never happened before. A soft knock on her chamber door broke her contemplation, and she crooked her finger slightly to open the door with magic. "Come, come."

Two elves, dressed in long white silk robes, helped the still badly wounded captain into the room, one of her legs still almost completely mangled. "Captain Ari'kel Everblade, Milady..." one of the elves started, but stopped at the queen's raised hand.

"I was under the assumption that this brave elf was to be healed," Tolandra said with a frown. "Was this not the case?"

"She *was* healed, My Queen," the other elf said with a tear rolling down her pale face. "I have never before seen anyone live through such...damage before."

"Leave us," Ari'kel said in a broken voice as she fell into a chair unceremoniously. Once the elves closed the doors, Ari'kel let out a small sob and tried to stand.

"Wait, dear warrior," Tolandra said, rushing to her side.

"No, My Queen. You have to hear this and no one else," Ari'kel said, clenching her teeth. "I will yet live, and this will haunt me for centuries." The captain stood, throwing her white hair back out of her bloodshot, violet eyes; eyes that were still black and bruised from the severe beating she had taken.

Queen Tolandra frowned and spun her hands, sending healing energy into the brave elven captain, despite her protests. She saw the light fighting against the wounds, almost like the rot that had affected Alant those many days ago in Dyln'ir. Finally, most of the wounds closed, and Ari'kel shuddered as she stood straighter.

"Thank you, My Queen," Ari'kel said with a tear. "Now hear the message I was saved to deliver two days ago, and I quote—*Tell your queen that I will await her in battle in the fields to the northwest of here. There she will face her doom.*"

"The fields of B'on," Tolandra whispered to herself more than anyone else. "And what was this foul creature who wiped out an entire elven guard?"

"He called himself Samor Cah, former Knight of Shad'ar."

"Former?"

"Yes, and truth be told, he had powers I have never heard of, even in children's fables," Ari'kel whispered as she sat down once more.

"Go on, brave warrior," the queen prompted. She had heard everything about this dark warrior from Evenal and Alant himself, and she wanted to know more before she went to meet him in battle.

"You're going to face him, aren't you?" Ari'kel asked with a note of terror in her voice.

"I am, but not without your knowledge of what happened and how he fought," the queen assured her. Tolandra stood and walked behind the chair, soothing Ari'kel and taking her long hair in her delicate hands. The Queen of all of Tsir'illia braided the fierce captain's hair—like they were young girls all over again—and listened intently as Ari'kel told her of the battle. The details were quite bothersome as it didn't sound at all like the Knights of Shad'ar she knew of or heard from Alant. A strategy occurred to the half-faerie queen as the tale unfolded, her mind racing furiously. She would need every bit of cunning and power at her disposal, although she was semi-confident that she could halt this menace at B'on.

Tolandra finished braiding Ari'kel's hair and realized the woman had fallen asleep. The queen poured more healing energy into the captain slowly, trying not to wake her. The woman had been in a fierce battle with Amara-only-knows-what, and she needed rest. The queen glided out of the room and shut the door, making a sign in the air to magically lock it so the captain wouldn't be disturbed.

"Lady, I..." one of the servants started to say, but stopped dead at the look the queen gave.

“Not now, Millicent,” Tolandra hissed, backing the lady-in-waiting up with her mere presence. “The captain is sleeping and *will not* be disturbed.” She eyed the older elf and tried not to smile, but failed. Millicent Whitetail had been serving her for as long as she could remember, and served her mother as well. The elf had to be almost seven hundred years old if she was ten.

“Understood, milady,” Millicent said, bowing low.

Tolandra walked briskly down the tower stairs to her personal armory, selecting the perfect staff and necklace for her daring plan. She was either going to win or die horribly; she couldn’t see any gray areas in this conflict. So be it, she thought as she set her jaw. *If I can rid the world of that evil with my life, then I will gladly do so.* Tolandra left quickly, using magic to get as close to the fields as she could; she would fly from there so as to observe this thing herself.

Field of B’on, Northern Tsir’illia.

He sat atop his undead steed and surveyed the field before him for any sign of an ambush. Not that he thought the elves could be that sneaky, but it never pays to underestimate your opponents. The fields of brown grass and rocks were situated high up above the coastline to the north, and small trees grew here and there. The brown grass seemed off somehow, but he paid it no mind; everything here would be dead soon anyway. Samor Cah swung his hammer lazily to one side as he waited for the queen. It had been four days since he sent that messenger, and he was getting impatient. He knew she would show up—she had to, at this point. He had called her out to her people—it was just a matter of when. The dark knight wasn't foolish—he knew this wasn't going to be an easy fight—but if he could slay her here and now, then the backbone of the elves would be broken.

Why do I still care about Raer'dreth's stupid war? he found himself thinking. *It's not like he did me any favors by bringing me back this time.* Samor looked down at his bone hand and wished for the hundredth time he could frown; it was impossible to do so, however, without a face. Samor shook his skull head to clear it of any lingering thoughts and looked around once more. He had to keep his mind on the task at hand lest he truly begin to hate what his former master had done to him.

Movement caught his unnatural sight, and his eyes flared green at the promise of battle. He was still trying to figure out his new powers, although he knew, now, that emotion fueled his fire within. Samor saw the queen come out of the forest on the opposite side, hovering three feet above the ground with her wings beating rapidly behind her as she held a staff with a glowing red ruby on the end of it. The fool of a woman wore no armor at all, only a long white robe, possibly made of silk. She stopped fifty yards from him and fingered a necklace made of emeralds.

"I am Queen Tolandra Asil, and I hear you wished to do battle with me, foul creature," she said with her back straight and her sapphire eyes narrowed.

Samor kicked his horse forward, walking it towards her slowly across the brown grass. "It is true, dear Queen," he answered. "I am Samor Cah, former Knight of Shad'ar and your doom on this day."

"You speak haughtily of things that have yet to pass, are you then a prophet?" Tolandra asked.

Samor could discern no sarcasm or deception in her voice. It was impressive that she would converse honorably before doing battle with him, and he found himself respecting this Queen of the Elves before him; pity she was going to die. “Prophet I am not, though I have been blessed with their handiwork in the past,” he said as he kept walking his horse toward her.

“Then you have great confidence in your new abilities, Lord Samor,” Tolandra said, raising her staff in the air as if to warn him.

Samor stopped the horse and tilted his head. “You know of my abilities before this?” he asked, genuinely intrigued.

“Oh yes. I have spoken to the young warrior who destroyed you and heard all about your powers,” the queen said as she started to circle the oncoming knight. “Alas, it is terrible to see you in this state, though. Does your existence pain you?”

Again, Samor could not discern anything other than her genuine curiosity. It almost sickened him. “Enough banter,” he growled as he pulled his hammer around. He kicked his horse into a gallop and charged the slender elven queen. “Now the elves fall.”

Tolandra flew up as Samor charged, and he brought the horse around hard, dirt spraying as its fiendish hooves dug in. He raised his shield as a ray of dark red blasted him from her staff, the force of which rocked him backward a bit. Had he been a normal man, he would have been unhorsed and possibly unconscious from that blast. He focused his anger and fired green rays from his eyes at her as she hovered in the air.

The queen grabbed her necklace and shouted a word in elven. “Triatha!” She cried as the green rays hit her, sending her flying backward in the air, head over wings. She righted herself and spread her wings out wide, the green blast held in a large sphere before her. She hurled it back at him, following it with a blast of red light from her staff.

Samor knew he was in trouble. He cocked his arm back and threw his hammer with all the strength he had as she sent his green rays back at him in sphere form. He saw the weapon smash into her just before he ducked behind his shield and braced himself. The concussion that followed flattened grass and trees alike for almost two hundred feet and sent him sprawling across the ground, tumbling a good hundred feet before he stopped in a heap of smoking armor and broken bones against a rock. His shield was completely rent, and his arm was broken in multiple places up to the shoulder. Samor stood and felt the gaping hole in his breastplate, burned away by his own powers—powers he couldn't feel at the moment.

"Not at rest yet?" the queen asked as she stood on shaky legs. Her robe was a mess of grass stains and blood, and his hammer lay at her feet. One of her arms was resting at an unnatural angle, and one wing was clearly ruined. She spat blood and smiled at him, clearly not out of the fight yet.

Samor was going to hurl a biting comment at her, but then he saw what was left of his horse and hung his head. "Damn. I liked that horse, too," he said. Samor raised his head high and walked towards the queen with determined steps. "No, I am not at rest," he said as he started picking up the pace, closing the distance quickly. "But you will be soon." He didn't have a weapon or a shield, but he was still strong. He waited for her to bring the staff around to fire the red blast and dodged under it, rolling, and coming up to his feet once more. He slammed his fist into her chest and heard bones snap, then kicked out and caught her in the stomach, sending her flying back into the grass near a broken tree.

Tolandra rolled over, vomiting blood. She used the staff for support and wove her fingers in a circle before making a fist. The brown grass sprang to life and entwined him, dragging him down to the ground.

“No! You will not contain me thus!” Samor fought and struggled with the enchanted grass, but just as he had almost broken free, a pillar of large rocks slammed into him from above and buried him. He tried to push them off, but with his ruined arm, it was pointless. Dirt started to fill in around the rocks, and soon he was completely entombed.

Tolandra vomited blood over the grass once more and dragged herself up onto a rock. She had buried the knight with rocks and then a wave of loose dirt that she had excavated with her magic. Her breath came in short bursts, and the pain was almost unbearable. Sobbing lightly, she made it to her feet and gathered her staff once more. *There is no way I can travel back with magic,* she thought. *I just don’t have it in me to cast a strong spell like that.* Yet the alternative would see her dead as well, as the journey home would take her days and, in this state, she didn’t have days. She could either use magic to heal herself—and it probably wouldn’t be enough to help her stay alive—or she could call for help.

She sat down heavily once more and let go of the staff, making gestures with her hands to send a message to Archmage Ereval. *He will never let me live this down*, she thought as she spat more blood upon the brown grass and laughed, wincing at the pain it caused. Tolandra couldn’t help but see the irony in this situation. The fields of B’on were supposed to be cursed by elven blood that was spilled centuries ago by a murderer. He had killed a young elven girl here in a forbidden ritual, a ritual that failed. He fled and was caught later, but the girl’s blood had tainted the land, turning the grass brown and making it so that no crops would fare well. “Well, add my blood to the mix,” Tolandra said out loud to no one in particular. She grabbed her throat where the enchanted necklace had been and thanked Amara that it had worked.

The Necklace of Syll was ancient and had been her mother’s before she had passed it to her. It was created by elves to catch magic and hurl it back at the original caster, but she wasn’t sure that his eyes would count. It had been destroyed in the process—leaving burns across her chest and neck—but it had saved her.

“My Lady!” Ereval called out as he stepped out of a portal near her tree. Ereval Drial was the Archmage of Dyln’ir and one of the most potent wizards in all of Tsir’illia. He had flowing white hair down his back and the most piercing violet eyes. His attire was white silk trimmed with gold, and a silver sash tied at the waist complemented the sword on his hip. He rushed to her side and wove his hands in the spell that would heal her enough so that she would survive.

“Thank Amara. Now get me home and into a nice warm bath,” Tolandra said as darkness started to form at the edge of her vision. “And I don’t want to hear about how I should…” Whatever else she was going to say was lost to the void as the darkness claimed her.

City of Llar, Southern Lorant.

She laughed and swung the man around her once again, stomping in time to the rhythm of the music echoing in the grand stone hall. It had been decades since she had last danced, and she had to admit that it was refreshing. Falgrim Ironhaft was a dwarven axe for hire and normally wouldn't be caught dead in a hall like this without some ale in her hand. She usually fixed most problems by hitting them, even when people said she shouldn't, *especially* when they said she shouldn't. Falgrim was a little over four feet tall and weighed enough to make her leathers creak when she sat. Her long hair was done in three long, black braids hanging down her back, and her traveling leathers—which were normally stained with a mixture of blood and dirt—had been exchanged for a set of fancy clothes. They tried to offer her a dress, but her scowl sent them running.

"I never thought you were the type for dancing," the man said as he spun around and wrapped his arms around her.

"What're you sayin'? I'm too cantankerous to dance?" Falgrim asked with a laugh. She still couldn't believe that she had fallen for this man—a human at that! Anatarn Blackblade had come into her life like an avalanche, swept up in a perilous run to take down a dark knight. He was a little over six feet tall with long black hair and dark eyes that made her frown less. He always dressed in all black and had a ridiculous black, wide-brimmed hat. The time they had spent on the road had brought them closer together, closer than Falgrim had been with any man in a very long time. They were closer than most folks could be...they were Heartbonded.

"Never!" Anatarn replied and kissed her on the top of the head. "Besides, I rather like my jaw right where it is."

"Have him trained already, eh, Falgrim?" another female dwarf asked as she danced by.

"Shut it, Belsa!" Falgrim laughed at her old friend. Belsa Harlow was a female dwarf with dirty blond hair and blue eyes. Belsa had always teased her relentlessly about men, and now was no exception.

A hearty laugh came from the corner; Falgrim saw her old friend Jimson, trying not to snort his ale. Jimson Stoutfist had brown hair, dark eyes, and a long brown beard, braided in three tails. He was a dwarven militia captain in Llar, and Falgrim had known him from way back. They had trained together before the war, and she thought of him like a brother.

The song ended, and they all cheered. They had been in the southern city of Llar for over a tenday now and had planned to leave days ago, but this festival had caught Falgrim's eye, so they were going to stay a couple more days. The Festival of Haav was a dwarven celebration of harvesting and renewal. Every year, they held one for the farmers and miners to set aside their tools and dance. Falgrim thought it would be a nice change and a perfect chance to spend time with Anatarn. *I should tell him about the bond...but I just can't,* she thought.

"So, you told me that you knew Jimson from before the war, but where did you meet Belsa?" Anatarn asked as they went to grab an ale.

Falgrim snorted and took an ale from him, downing most of it in one swig. "I met Belsa during the Brenshin War. We both served in the 3rd Silver Regiment, I was second axe and she was third axe," Falgrim said as she thought back to those days. The Brenshin War was brutal and bloody; even to this day, dwarves are looked at with disdain and contempt in some places.

"Ah, that makes sense, then," Anatarn said with a wry smile.

"What does?"

"The fact that you two are always bickering, even in jest. You were her superior, she has never forgotten that."

Falgrim stared at Anatarn with shock. For a human to know how dwarves think was bad enough, but to have him figure this out was unheard of. "How do you know that?"

"I went through a lot of counseling after the war, and the dwarven priest who helped me had explained a lot of things to me," Anatarn said with a smile.

"I'm sorry," Falgrim said, turning away and hiding her frown. She hated bringing up the war with him for this very reason. Anatarn had been married to a dwarf, and he had lost her in the war.

"Never be sorry," he said, laying his hand on her shoulder and turning her around to face him. "That is part of my past, just like you are a part of my future. They all make me who I am." He kissed her on the top of the head and leaned in to whisper. "He even explained what a Heartbond is."

Before Falgrim could say anything, the door burst open and two soldiers came hustling in towards Jimson. "Captain, come quick!"

"What is it?" Jimson asked, pulling his axe from his baldric.

"A lone dwarf child, Lanni Hoarfren of Harvon, says a black knight is coming with a hoard of monsters. She is a mess, sir, and, well...we believe her."

"Take me to her," Jimson said with a grim look on his face.

"We're coming too," Anatarn said, pulling Falgrim behind him. "I want to hear about this black knight."

Falgrim was in shock that Anatarn had said that, but right now the sinking feeling in her gut—and her gut was never wrong—was telling her they should have left and run north while they had a chance. They didn't go far before they could see other guards sitting with a small dwarf girl, covered in dirt and grime, her tear-streaked face a mask of horror.

"Alright, Lass, tell me what is going on," Jimson said, going down to one knee in front of the little one.

"It's hard to cry when you're angry," the girl said, almost like she was in a trance.

"She's been saying that ever since they left to get you, Captain," another dwarf replied.

Anatarn slowly dropped to both knees on the opposite side of the little one, his voice barely a whisper. "Black armor, made of smoke," the warrior said.

"And glowing eyes of fire...you've seen it too?" The dwarf girl had true fear in her wide eyes as she focused on Anatarn

"Tell us all of it, Lanni," Jimson said as he covered her with a blanket. "Leave nothing out."

Lanni took a deep breath and started crying as she talked. "It was by the edge of the desert, in the Forest of Dust, north of Harvon. I *know* we weren't supposed to go that far into the woods, but we were just having fun."

"We?" Falgrim asked as that pit in her stomach grew to be the size of a watermelon.

"My brother, Danni...that thing killed him with that awful, burning ash from the sword," Lanni said as she looked up at Falgrim and Anatarn.

"What about the monsters?" Jimson asked, getting the girl back to the story before she broke down further.

"The dead. They were just walking right out of the sand, and the dark knight was leading them. It was horrifying to see skeletons walking like that, sand coming out of their mouths and eye sockets...then it saw us."

"Callen Drah," Anatarn said as he stood, putting a name to the horror for the rest of the gathered dwarves.

"You know what it is, don't you?" Lanni asked, her voice quivering now.

"Yes, sadly, I do know what it is," Anatarn replied with a hard edge to his voice now.

"Can you do me a favor then?" The dwarf girl's eyes hardened suddenly, like a smith's anvil.

"What is it, Lass?" Falgrim asked, laying her hand on the girl's shoulder.

"Kill it for me? Kill it for Danni?"

"That is something I am certainly going to try to do, Lanni," Anatarn swore. He turned to a dwarf guard and smiled, the mirth never touching his eyes. "Make sure this one is taken care of; I have a dark knight to dismember." Anatarn strode off, pulling Falgrim in his wake.

Normally, Falgrim would have argued and pulled his arm out of his socket for treating her like this, but she knew where it was coming from. "An," she called out to him as they walked. When she got nothing back, she set her feet and tugged slightly to get his attention. "Anatarn."

"What, Lass?" he asked, almost surprised at why she was calling him.

"We'll get him, don't worry, but take it easy tugging me like that. I told you I like it rough, but not when we're walking," Falgrim said, smiling at him.

"Sorry, I just want to find Eliyan and get going. That monster could be in Harvon already. It must've taken the girl forever to get here." Anatarn turned and pulled Falgrim in for a warm embrace. "Forgive me?"

"Of course. Now, let's go find that prissy little elf and get going before the other hammer falls."

"I haven't heard that saying in forever," Anatarn said as he laughed.

"You're taking a platoon of guards as well," Jimson said, coming over to them. "And they will be led by me."

Falgrim patted her old friend on the back and spit in the dirt. "Good. Now let's go stomp this thing out for good."

CHAPTER FOUR — THE HAMMER FALLS

Border Bridge, Branthian/Lorant Border

Syn'ella was in awe of her surroundings. They had traveled to Fort Yarin and warned the Knight-Commander there about the dead, and with the backing of Lieutenant Haves, they were given fresh horses, some smoked fish, and even a ship to cross the Illian lake to speed their journey. It had been two days of new experiences, and between that and her new bond with Alant, the little faerie was going to explode. She still couldn't believe that she and Alant were soulbonded, something that she had only dreamed about.

Syn'ella had always been a hopeless romantic, and the stories of elves being bonded like that had always interested her. Now, however, she was actually living it. The bond between them was intense, always letting her know where he was and how he was doing. She could even concentrate and find out which direction he was in if she focused hard enough.

“Just a couple more feet and we’re in Lorant,” Alant said from behind her.

Syn’ella leaned back into him as they rode and smiled at the warm feeling his closeness gave her. She had initially been worried that he would want a human girl—someone his own size, at least, since she was only two and a half feet tall—but he had shown her that he was hers alone. “I’m glad I get to experience these things with you, Alant,” Syn’ella said as she lightly flipped the reins again. He had even taught her how to control the horse with these weird contraptions.

“And I with you, Love,” the young man replied.

Before she could say anything else, a wagon came into view up ahead—the smoke from a small fire could be seen lifting into the evening sky. “Hey, look,” Syn’ella said, sitting up and handing the reins to Alant.

“Looks like a merchant wagon from Lorant,” Alant said as he pulled the horse to a stop. Strange place to camp, though.”

“Hail there, rider,” a sturdy dwarf said. He was all of four feet tall—and almost as wide—with a wide-brimmed hat trimmed with gold and a long mustache curled up at the ends. The dwarf stood and placed his hand on the haft of his axe that hung at his side, yet made no move to draw it. His smile was genuine, but wary as his eyes scanned to the left and right of them. “Just you two then?”

Alant dismounted and held his hands out before him. “Just the two of us, yes,” he replied, “We are traveling to Lorant on a diplomatic mission for Branthian.”

“Oho! A diplomat, and with a fae companion at that,” the dwarf said with a hearty chuckle. “Haven’t ever seen one of the fae with me own eyes before.”

Syn’ella growled softly. The term fae was not well-liked by her people, as it conjured horrible images that related to their dark cousins. They had banished those terrible faeries many centuries ago, long before the war had even started, yet the stories haunted them ever since. Stories of sneaking into homes and stealing human children, sacrificing them to gain power, made her sick thinking about those dark times.

"And I, good sir, have never beheld one of the stout folk," Syn'ella said, unfurling her wings as she stood in the saddle. She glared at the dwarf, knowing that he probably didn't know, but irritated all the same.

"Aye, well said, and I'm sorry if the term fae was offensive, milady," the dwarf said with a low bow. "The name's Haragrym Wordsplitter, or just Grym, to me friends."

"Thank you, Grym," Syn'ella said, inclining her head in respect. She saw Alant looking at her curiously and sighed. "I am Syn'ella, and this is Silverlord Alant Landsaver."

"Silverlord?"

"It's a new title in Branthian, but never mind," Alant said with a slight blush.

Syn'ella giggled and smiled widely. "Maybe I can tell you the story of the dark fae as we share your fire?"

"We have some smoked fish from our last stop, and we would be happy to split it with you," Alant offered as well.

"Aye, that sounds fair. I always trade a good tale for company. Come, Alant and Syn'ella, and rest your legs from the long ride." Grym turned and stalked back to his fire, patting the two horses near his covered wagon.

Syn'ella could see that the back of his wagon was like a small room, and she wondered where he kept his wares, which he was peddling. *Maybe he is not a merchant, after all,* she thought, feeling overly curious. She flew over behind the wagon and looked at Grym first for approval.

"Oh, go ahead and peek. I have always heard that the fa...I mean, faerie folk were curious to a fault," Grym said, laughing. "I have no secrets to keep."

Syn'ella smiled and flew into the wagon, looking around in awe at the furnishings. The inside of the wagon was lavish, with a braided rug on the floor and hangings of carved animals dangling from the support beams. Crates of clothes and books lined the edges of the wagon, with a bed of hay was lined with wood in the far end. It was like his own room at an inn. There were more books by the bed, with several dozen lined on makeshift shelves.

"Ye like me books, fair one?"

"I have never seen so many books outside of a library before," Syn'ella admitted. "Do you sell them?"

"I sell them, yes," Grym said with a sly wink.

His answer made her wrinkle her nose in thought. He was saying something with his vague answer—something she missed. She looked back at the books, and then she saw it. Most of the books had his name on them! "Oh, my Goddess, you write them?"

Grym bowed low and swept his hat off in a grand gesture, climbing into the wagon himself after replacing his hat. "Why, yes, I do. All manner of books on valiant battles, honorable heroes, and brave deeds."

"Oh, great," Alant said, coming over. He had the package of smoked fish in one hand and a bottle of wine in the other. "Now she won't stop telling stories all night."

"'Tis fine by me, young Silverlord. I revel in a good tale, be it true or not."

"Oh, it's true, we've been fighting the risen dead, black knights of myth, and a war is coming to Branthian," Syn'ella said as she flew out and kissed Alant on the top of the head.

"The risen dead, you say?" Grym said with a frown. His happy demeanor vanished in a blink, replaced with a troubling look indeed.

“What is it, good dwarf?” Alant asked with a serious tone.

“I’ve heard rumors of the dead walking through the forests to the east of here, but I thought it was just folk seeing things. If it is true that you’ve fought them, then mayhap they are heading for the outlying villages.” Grym leapt down and started kicking the fire, stomping the embers out and rushing to the horses. “I’m sorry, folks, but I have no time to rest and hear your tale this night. I have to warn the good folk of Lorant.”

“And you won’t do it alone,” Alant promised as he drew Ilen’dar. The sword gave off a faint hum that echoed across the grass.

“Yeah, we’ll come with you and save the people!” Syn’ella said, drawing her own tiny blade.

“Now this will make a fine tale in and of itself,” Grym said as he gathered his supplies. “Let us ride like the wind!”

Syn’ella flew up onto the horse and kissed Alant quickly on the lips as he mounted. “For luck,” she said, as she always did these days when they kissed—she knew life could be fleeting. In moments, they were riding across the grasslands, following the wagon as it bounced and jostled down the road at a speed they never thought a wagon could attain.

City of Llar, Southern Lorant.

The elf smiled as she handed the dress to the young dwarven girl, ignoring the stares of the mother that had been burning into her back for almost an hour. Eliyan Safril was an elven wizard of the House Safril and Niece to the Queen of Tsir'illia herself. She looked young—even for an elf—and wore a dress of diaphanous silk. Her long white hair was entwined with lilacs, and she wore a golden sash around her waist. Her deep violet eyes contained a weight, though, one like she had seen the depths of the hells and knew what was awaiting them all. Eliyan had been saved by Falgrim and Anatarn and had joined them in Llor, fleeing that city and coming south to escape the dark knight that pursued them.

"You missed a spot," the gruff dwarven mother mumbled.

Eliyan sighed and smiled wider, taking the garment back from the young lass and twisting her fingers once more in the cleaning spell. To explain that magic couldn't "miss a spot" was futile. The dwarves distrusted the elves' use of magic and always would.

"Mother, it was perfectly fine," the young lass insisted.

"Snuff it, Killen." The mother harrumphed and walked away.

Killen turned and smiled at Eliyan. I'm sorry for me ma, she is just a grumpy old sort." Killen Everstone was short and stout, with long braided brown hair and deep grey eyes.

"I know. It's alright, young one," Eliyan said, grabbing an apron this time. She had wanted to make herself useful while they were in Llar and help where she could, so she volunteered at the local wash house and used her magic to clean the clothes of the workers.

"Still funny to hear you say that," Killen said with a snort. "Hard to believe you're that much older than me."

"I will be ninety-one winters this year, very young among wizards in the land of Tsir'illia," Eliyan said plainly. It wasn't until Killen rolled her eyes that she heard how that must've sounded. "I'm sorry. I was raised in a royal house, so

I've not had much practice seeming humble before. I must seem very condescending."

"I admit you seem a little high and mighty, but I can say that it isn't true the way you cast magic like that," Killen said with a bit of awe in her voice. "I've seen sorcerers before, and you make magic look like breathing compared to them."

"That's just it," Eliyan admitted with a wink. "It *is* like breathing to us. I've been working magic for over half my life, so close to forty years now."

"Blah blah blah, you're old. We know," a gruff voice broke in from the door.

"Nice axe!" Killen said, standing and staring with wide eyes.

Falgrim pushed right by the young dwarven girl. "Shut it, kid. Let's go, Eliyan, time to kill a dark knight."

Eliyan had seen that determined look on the dwarf's face before; it still gave her nightmares. So, too, did the image of that dark knight that had hunted for her. "You found her?" The elf's voice quivered slightly, and she tried to stiffen her back and not faint.

"Yeah. She killed a kid in the Forest of Dust northwest of here. We're heading out in an hour; come with me so we can get you some gear or whatever it is you need." Falgrim grabbed Eliyan by the wrist and pulled her out of the wash house.

A large group of dwarven militia was sitting in the street, mounted on ponies with Jimson at the head as well as Anatarn. The tall human warrior was all smiles and black leather with that wide-brimmed hat of his. "Sorry to cut it short, but it's two days to the forest, and who knows how far this army of the dead has gotten?"

"Army of the dead?!" Eliyan asked as her eyes went wide. I leave you two alone for three days, and you have an army of the dead?"

"We'll explain on the way. Hey, maybe your magic will come in handy for once," Falgrim chided her.

"We don't need my magic as long as you have that anger and your axe," Eliyan replied with a smirk. She was learning that Falgrim liked to pick on her and that she didn't detest her as much as she had initially feared. Now she was getting good at poking the dwarven axe-for-hire right back and it seemed to have brought them closer.

"She's not wrong," Anatarn said with a laugh. "Let's ride!"

Eliyan pushed down the feeling of terror that the dark knight had brought back. Back in Llor, she stood against the dark knight with her magic and did well, but once the moment passed, the fear hit her right in the stomach. *I know I have to face my fear, but that woman scares the white out of my hair*, she said to herself.

Castle Wrath, Isle of Raer'drin.

He breathed in the stale air of his workroom, leaning on a huge marble table in the center with three empty high-backed chairs around it. The room was big, with a massive circular hole in the ceiling showing the brilliant night sky. This hole was shielded by an invisible spell that kept out the elements, yet allowed him a gorgeous view of the fathomless stars above. Other, smaller slabs lay around the edges of the room with dozens of crystal stands containing soul gems, gemstones that were made to house the souls of his warriors and keep them from the afterlife. All of his Knights of Shad'ar were gone now, sailing on ships that would enact the dark war he had been planning ever since he was exiled by his brethren all those many years ago.

Archmage Raer'dreth Iliad took a deep breath and let it out slowly, as one gemstone drew his eye. It was cracked and pulsated with a sickly green light as opposed to the other soft blue lights. Even as he watched it, the stone flickered and surged, indicating that the soul of the knight attached to it was in danger.

Ah, Samor, what have you gotten yourself into now? the archmage thought as he walked over slowly to the cracked stone. His dark robe dragged on the stone floor behind him as he studied the receptacle with a critical eye. His Knights of Shad'ar were all undead souls tied to these pulsating soul gems—prisons for their very souls. If they were slain in battle, their souls would flee here to rest in the soul gems and wait to be reborn once more in the dead body he sent them into, the fresher the better. Raer'dreth had never before had one that had been slain outright until Samor Cah's soul had been severed from his spell by that upstart warrior-child.

Raer'dreth shook his head as he remembered how hard it was to call that soul back from the land of the dead, fighting like an angler on a ship in heavy seas, reeling in a huge catch. The archmage had been successful—if you could call it that—and had sent Samor's soul into the land of the living once more, but unguided this time. The stories had always been there, warnings from Shar'in—Goddess of Death and Shadows—when he had made the pact with her and gained his dark powers. He had honestly never given them much heed until now.

Raer'dreth lifted his hands and made twin gestures with both hands, calling on his magic to send a magical compulsion into the stone, hoping that this time it would take. When he first called Samor back, he couldn't get a good hold on the soul, so it had been on its own until now. The dark archmage could feel the hatred and pain of Samor; still, he could not wrap the compulsion around that tortured soul to control him once more.

I feel you, my former master, Samor sent across the ether, echoing in the archmage's head. *I will not be controlled by you anymore.* The voice carried pain and rage, laced with loathing.

You are mine, Samor Cah, and you always will be, Raer'dreth sent back with a surge of power to hold the undead warrior fast. Instead, his magic hit a wall of force, a green flare in his mind as his spells bounced back on him.

Raer'dreth flinched as all his muscles went rigid at once, his own magic locking him in place. He seethed inside his mind as he waited for the magic to fade, helpless at resisting his spells. Someone else had been giving Samor his powers, and if it was who he thought it was, then the shadowknight was completely out of his grasp forever; he would have to destroy him. Raer'dreth stumbled, gripping the smaller stone slab for balance as the magic ceased. Raer'dreth looked to Samor's soul gem, and the flickering light was solid and pulsating once more. Whatever had happened to the former shadowknight, he was healed and back in the game. "If that is you, oh great Shar'in, then I hope your plans do not impede my own," he said aloud to the night sky as he walked back to the marble table and sat in one of the chairs. Raer'dreth knew that to go against the wishes of his goddess was probably suicide, but he had come too far to concede victory, even to one such as her.

"Well, if you want something done right..." Raer'dreth said aloud as he stood, walking briskly to his chambers. He selected a dark robe from his wardrobe and a golden rope belt. He gathered some of his most prized items and hooked them onto this belt as he prepared for something he hadn't done in an exceedingly long time; he was going home. The archmage stopped and looked at himself in his floor-length mirror, his robe swirling behind him as he turned. He had a small rod, a clawed, withered hand, and an orb in a leather holder attached to his belt. He grabbed two ancient books and slid them into his black, leather sling bag, the tomes disappearing into the swirling void of the magic bag. They were as old as he was and contained something he had used only once, a spell so deadly that it made him smile just thinking of what it would do to his enemies. *I'll have the twins send over the soul gems once I get in and set up,* he thought as he walked to his workroom once more, ready to use the corridors of magic to take him to Alian'tir and certain victory.

They both collapsed on the cold stone floor, their combined magic fading fast as the bowl of components dissolved, consumed by the magic ritual. Ril and Xil had merged their magic as one, blocking their father from Samor Cah, just as they had foreseen in their vision.

"If he ever..." Xil started, but Ril held up a finger, silencing him.

"He won't, as long as we're careful. You saw what I did all those years ago. This is the only way," Ril said as he stood and dusted off his robe, trying to get his breathing under control.

Xil nodded, getting up and grabbing the table for balance. "It's one thing to have visions, but to actually be a part of them is a little disorienting."

"I agree, come, let's grab some food and rest."

"So, what do we do now, brother?" Xil asked, a slow smile spreading on the half-elf's face. "Should we contact the ships?"

“Not yet. We have to save our strength for later...we’ll need it.” Ril walked to the window where he could see the entire city below them. The people had seen their power now and knew who they were. *It is almost time.*

Fields of B’on, Northern Tsir’illia

A fist broke through the ground, grabbing the boulder and shoving it aside. Samor Cah rose from the ground, fully whole and ready to kill anything in his path. He had won a contest of wills against his former master and had felt a presence in his mind aiding him. That presence was powerful—beyond anything he had ever felt in a long time. It made even Raer’dreth’s powers seem small in comparison. Someone was giving Samor his chance for freedom. *Could it be the goddess?* he wondered

“Oh, mighty Shar’in, your will shall be done,” Samor Cah said to the night sky as he stood across the empty fields of B’on ready for the coming battle. His eyes flared with green light—not a beam of fire this time, but a sickly illumination. It showed a trail of magic, floating through the air towards the northwest. The dark knight knew his destination now, and woe to any that got in his way.

CHAPTER FIVE — SACRIFICES MADE

Capital City of Llor, Nation of Lorant

She stood on her balcony and smiled despite the tension swirling through her life. She knew what had to be done—they had talked around every possibility, but it always came down to the same thing. Alsan breathed a heavy sigh, tightened her night robe against the chill in the air, and turned to her latest bedroom conquest—a conquest that had lasted days instead of one night. "Alright, Ongril, let's do it."

"The rest of my retinue has already sent word to the lesser nobles, Lady Brenshin," the elf said as he came towards her. His slender arms enfolded her lovingly as he kissed her neck under her ear, biting playfully at her lobe. "The lesser nobles will have all their guards converge on the throne room when my signal is seen over the square." Ongril Silvertree was an elven steward of Tsir'illia, serving Eliyan Safril, but he had been with Alsan ever since she had met him, just outside the king's chambers. They had been discussing high treason for days; that and dancing amidst the silk sheets.

"You knew I would eventually cave, didn't you?" Alsan asked as she ran her fingers through his white hair.

"I did. It is the only course of action to take, milady."

"I still think we will all die horribly," Alsan confessed. "Yet there is truly no other way to bring the light back to Lorant." Alsan pulled Ongril's hair back, staring directly into his emerald eyes. "Why do you still insist on calling me 'milady' after all we've done together these past nights?

"Are you not a lady?" Ongril teased, running his hands down to her hips, never breaking away from her gaze.

"Courtly etiquette runs in your very blood, doesn't it fair elf?" Alsan asked playfully, pushing him away and turning to the side. She had never felt freer than when she was here with this elf that had crashed into her life. Most men she had taken to her chambers were shallow or even despicable. She had her fun, and they were on their way, usually with some consequence that would infuriate her brother, or her father when he was alive. This one, however, had pushed his way into her heart and made her feel whole and pure, for the first time since she was a very young girl. *I could almost tell him my secret, yet I fear to,* she thought as she stared at him.

"When that is all you do for close to sixty years..." Ongril inclined his head and laughed at the face Alsan made at that. "I know, it is hard to imagine that I am over one hundred and forty winters, but it is so."

Alsan recovered from the shock quickly, her years at etiquette serving her well. "I always knew I liked older men, but this is taking it a bit too far," Alsan said, walking behind her wardrobe. She let her robe fall and selected a white silk dress, laced with gold trim and a sash of green leaves on a silver background. She stepped back out a couple of minutes later to see Ongril dressed as well, his white silk clothes immaculate and pressed. "By the Gods above, you look handsome."

“Thank you, milady,”

Alsan’s smile faded as reality came crashing back down on her. “The fact that my brother would make a pact with such evil makes me sick. Albron will pay for all the deaths caused by that dark knight.”

“Well said, milady. Now let us go...we have treason to carry out.” Ongril strode to the door and held it open for her, bowing slightly as she crossed the threshold. There was no turning back now, and though he was terrified to his core, he knew that he had finally found his purpose in his long life—advisor to the Queen of Lorant.

Alsan walked with confidence down the many hallways, dressed for court when there was none scheduled. This drew many eyes to her—as they both had hoped it would—and soon she had a small following behind her as she approached the throne room. She saw Ongril break off and take the circular stairs to the left, keeping his head down. *Good luck, my love*, Alsan thought as she kept walking towards the throne room. It wasn’t unheard of for her to barge in on her brother. What *was* unheard of was her doing it without first announcing herself to the castle steward, so they knew she was coming.

The guards outside the throne room crossed their spears and set their feet squarely when they saw her approaching. “You are not expected this morn, Lady Brenshin. Turn around and find the steward if you want an audience.”

“Guards, Albron is my brother,” Alsan said without slowing down one bit. “I will talk to him, or you can strike a member of the royal family; pick one.”

The people following her slowed and moved to the side of the grand hallway, whispering amongst themselves. The guards looked at the people, then back at Alsan, before pulling their spears back at the last second.

"Good boys," Alsan said as she pushed the doors open. She hesitated there for a second, turning to them and smiling. "Now, if you want to live after today...I would go and have a pint at the tavern; trouble is coming." She walked into the throne room, leaving the doors wide open.

"What is the meaning of this, Alsan?" Albron said as he stood near his throne. The entire throne room was shrouded in dim light as more than half of the torches had burned down and had turned black. There were two strange warriors next to the king who seemed like bounty hunters, and they eyed her with malice as she approached. Her brother kept to the shadows, ignoring her with practiced ease.

"I am here to plead with you one final time, Albron," Alsan said as she slowed down. These warriors weren't part of their plan, and she had to think quickly. "You're my brother, and I have to try."

"I am not in the mood for your childish games, Alsan!" the king spat, venom on his tongue as sure as she had ever heard it. "Now turn around before I have my new friends throw you out," Albron finished, turning away from her and whispering to one of the warriors.

Alsan was taken aback by his venomous words. It was then she realized there were no guards in the throne room at all. "Where are the guards, Albron?" she asked hesitantly. Alsan hoped that these two weren't seasoned fighters, as the lesser nobles' guards had the numbers but not the skill. If these two held the doors before they could breach the throne room, all could be lost. Alsan squared her shoulders and walked forward. She had, of course, been trained to fight as a member of the royal family, but it had been years since she had bothered with any of it. She had to think of some way to keep them near the throne longer.

"The guards were plotting against me, sister. They have been dealt with." Albron finally stepped out of the shadows, walking down the throne steps and facing his sister.

Alsan stopped dead, her hand flying to her mouth to stifle a scream. "Brother...what have you done?" Alsan dropped to her knees in shock and horror as she saw his face. His eyes were burned away!

Albron reached the floor and stopped, tilting his head. His shaggy hair was lopped off, and his eyes looked like he had taken a torch to them, the burns reaching across his face. "I was seeing things, shadows dancing across the ceiling, so I fixed it. Now, nothing can frighten me or distract me," Albron said with a small laugh as he leaned down to her. His visage was twisted in a hideous grin.

Alsan choked on despair. Her brother was gone now, she could see that. His mind fractured and twisted into madness and despair. She could hear faint, distant cheers and knew it was now or never. She had to get him away from the throne and his guards. "Albron, I am truly sorry." Alsan reached up and grabbed her brother, turning and flipping him over her shoulder, sending him tumbling down the stone steps away from the throne.

Albron screamed and thrashed on the steps as he tumbled to the cold stone floor. He drew his hidden dagger and got to his knees. "Kill her!"

Ongril took the stairs quickly, trying to focus on the task at hand. This was harder than he thought it would be, as his mind drifted continuously to Alsan's safety. *Get it together and stay*

on track, he berated himself as he found the small balcony he needed. There was only one guard, and she seemed rather bored.

"Excuse me, fair lady," Ongril said as he approached meekly. "But I'm worried for the king."

"What're you babbling about, twig?" the woman asked, pulling her spear around and looking down at him.

"I saw a small force of people heading towards the throne room. They didn't look at all friendly." Ongril was adept at this sort of thing. It wasn't lying, per se, but reimaging the truth. It always made him seem genuine. The guard grunted and took off down the stairs, leaving him free to step out onto the balcony and look out over the city.

As Ongril took a deep breath, he could see dark clouds rolling in overhead, the promise of a storm imminent. He closed his eyes and focused on the magic, curling his fingers into a fist and bringing his spell to life. All elves knew magic to some extent—it flowed through their blood since time began—but the strength of that magic differed in every elf. Ongril wasn't very powerful at all, only being able to control the very basics of some spells and effects. Normally, he would never bother, as his spells were ineffectual in most scenarios...today, however, he was proud to be able to do this.

Ongril looked out over the distant square, a square that had been drenched in the blood of all the high nobles not very long ago. His smile widened as he saw the bright light form over the square, illuminating the abandoned carts and shining into the homes around for two blocks. That was his specialty; he could call light with his magic. The signal was sent, and Ongril could hear a faint cheer rise up in the distance. It would take the nobles a few minutes to get here, but hopefully the throne room would be open, and everything would go as planned. He rushed back down the stairs, taking them two at a time, and flew towards the throne room. He saw the two guards, as well as the one he sent down, walking away, shaking their heads.

"If she says to run, I'm listening," one guard told the other two.

"Yeah, the king killed his personal guards for laughing at a joke...I don't want any part of this any longer." The three guards walked out and turned the corner; Ongril breathed a sigh of relief. The plan was working for once. Then he heard the king scream.

"Kill her!"

Fear almost rooted Ongril to the spot, but he fought the despair and ran on, his heart beating so hard he could almost hear it out loud. He saw the throne room doors open, and all the people cowering in fear to the sides of the grand hallway. The throne room seemed dark and dim, a sure reflection of the battle ahead if he ever saw one. A moment of clarity made him stop running and swallow; he was meant to be here.

Fate was a strange thing that many elves believed in, yet he was never one for it. Your life was what you made of it, or so he always thought. Now, though, Ongril could feel it—his purpose. He shot his fist forward and curled his fingers, calling forth light into the throne room. Ongril closed his eyes and walked forward, his fist outstretched before him as light blossomed inside the throne room again and again in various places. Though elves never needed spoken words for their magic, something inside compelled him to speak this time. "Let the light surround you, Alsan!" Ongril cried out as the blossoming light exploded, forcing the two strange men back away from his love, blinded as the king tumbled away, covering his face.

"Ongril!" Alsan cried out, rushing towards him as the light filled the room.

"I'm here, Alsan. I will always be here." Ongril said as they heard shouts coming from the grand hallway.

The guards of the lesser nobles had stormed the castle, and fighting could now be heard everywhere. The lesser nobles themselves were leading the charge, knowledge of what had happened to the other nobles spurring them on. They spilled past Alsan and Ongril, taking the king and placing him under arrest while also taking out the strange warriors. Ongril's light shone brightly as they cheered, the darkness washing away from the throne as Alsan cried silently in Ongril's arms.

Village of Harvon, Nation of Lorant

The platoon of dwarves pulled up when Anatarn raised his fist—a silent command to halt. They had marched double-time to the village of Harvon in hopes of catching this army of the dead before anyone else was overrun. Zomnus—God of Luck and Fate—was with them as the village was, as yet, untouched.

"Have these people get going," Anatarn told Jimson as they gathered everyone around. "I'm heading in there to scout ahead."

"No, ye are not," Falgrim said, stepping in front of Anatarn. She had her hands on her wide hips, and her eyes blazed with challenge. "You will be going with me or not at all."

Anatarn rolled his eyes but smiled. "Alright, I'll wait, but let's get these people going." He turned to the gathering crowd of humans and dwarves as Jimson sent troops around the village to knock on homes.

"Good citizens of Harvon. We need you to please move to the southeast gate and prepare to travel. Do not pack or bring anything you don't absolutely need. This is an emergency, and it is for your safety." Anatarn could see the fear in their faces, and he hated telling them like this, but they had no time.

"You heard 'im! Let's go!" Jimson roared to snap them out of their stupor.

The organized chaos that followed faded quickly as the small company left and gathered in the woods north of the village. Anatarn, Eliyan, and Falgrim stood and looked out at the serene forest with trepidation, the awkward silence stretching until finally Falgrim broke it.

"What's the play?" Falgrim asked solemnly as she took her axe off her back and hefted it a couple of times to get the feel of it. She never had to do this—the thing was like another arm to her at this point—but it was something she always did.

"Kill anything that isn't us?" Anatarn answered with a smile.

As if that was the cue fate needed to hear, the enemy came into view as they shambled through the trees. The dead were shuffling and stomping over the roots and through the bushes, many of them missing bones, and some of them missing parts of their face and jaw. Sand still slowly trickled out of their eyes and mouth as they were jostled by the trees they tried to avoid. Their tattered clothes were ripped and stained with filth and blood, swaying in the breeze that also brought their wicked smell. There were hundreds of them!

"Form up," Anatarn said, but he wasn't quick enough.

Falgrim was off the minute she saw them, barreling around the trees and swinging her axe in wide arcs. She dropped one, then another, but the first one reached up and grabbed her ankle as it crawled after her, holding her fast in its bone-strengthened grip. Falgrim hacked at the arm, but that left her open to the one who was getting up. The curved sword came down quickly...only to be met by the black blade of Anatarn.

"Why do you rush to your death?" Anatarn asked calmly. He dispatched the one in front as she slammed the one holding her. "Is it to impress me?"

"Shut it." Falgrim swung again, taking down another—but three more replaced that one. "They're fighting dirty by not dying."

"Sounds logical," Eliyan said, coming behind them and crossing her fingers, then bringing them down. A strong wind came howling behind the heroes and blew the dead back two paces, enough room for Anatarn to swing Dark and sever three of them. The sword went clean through them and they didn't get back up. "After all, they are dead already. Why do something twice, right?"

Falgrim looked back at the elf and scowled, then laughed. "You're learning girly. We'll have you insulting others like a proper dwarf in no time."

Anatarn smiled, but he knew they were already in trouble. They had dropped a mere handful, and there were hundreds. Plus, he hadn't seen Callen Drah yet. "We have to fall back, Falgrim. Back to the village, I think," he said as he parried two curved swords and ducked a third before killing another. His sword was taking them out somehow...he just wished he knew how. *Damn magical swords,* he thought as he back-stepped and parried another. *Why can't they just tell you how they work?*

"I'll signal Jimson," Falgrim said, taking off a horn she had brought and putting it to her lips. The dwarf blew three hard, clarion blasts that echoed across the woods, then stuffed the horn in her belt and swung her axe again as she backed up.

"Eliyan, go," Anatarn said. "Tell Jimson the dead are coming while Falgrim and I hold them back a bit."

The elf nodded and turned, running through the trees with ease, not even one branch touching her pale skin.

"I hate elves sometimes," Falgrim said as she watched her leave.

"Sometimes?" Anatarn laughed as more dead poured around the trees after them. "Falgrim, I do believe you are showing personal growth."

"Just keep killing and shut up." Falgrim stumbled and blocked a curved sword, then swore as her ankle twisted. She hit a tree and cried out, using her axe to lean on.

"I've got you," Anatarn said as his strong arms enfolded her waist and lifted the weight off her foot.

"I'll be fine, just swing yer damned sword." Falgrim pushed him off and stood, biting down the pain.

Anatarn frowned and cleared a path back to the village. They had only walked an hour into the woods, but the fight back took almost three times as long, and he was getting tired. By the time he cleared the trees, he could see that the dead were actually flanking them, the sounds of battle ringing clear from the village. He blocked and parried as they fell back, shouting for Jimson the whole way. With a horrible realization, Anatarn knew why no one had answered the call from Falgrim's horn once he stumbled backwards into the main square.

The dead were everywhere. The entire platoon was fragmented, small pockets trying in vain to hold back the tide of dead that seemed intent on slaying them all. The dead were surrounding them and picking them off while there, on a small cart, stood Callen Drah. Standing proud in her shadowy armor, her flame eyes burned brightly as she watched the dead take them down one at a time.

“Get me a clear shot,” Falgrim said as she limped behind him towards a pocket of dwarves. “Just one shot.”

“I’ll try, Falgrim.” Anatarn swung wildly now, his arms aching and sweat pouring into his eyes. How these dwarves held onto their stamina had always amazed him. He kicked out at one and swung Dar’kir in a low arc, taking four dead in the legs, tumbling them against each other. “Now, Falgrim.”

Falgrim spun and let her axe fly with both hands, the weapon tumbling end over end through the air towards the dark knight.

This time, however, Callen wasn’t surprised by the attack. She dodged aside as the axe sailed by, embedding itself in a wall. “Now you will fall, dwarf—alone and weaponless in the dirt,” Callen said, as she lowered her arm in Falgrim’s direction.

Falgrim spun and kicked, but her foot betrayed her. She fell, the dead piling on top of her.

“Falgrim!” Anatarn was there, pulling the dead off and slicing through them, yet more came at them. He took hit after hit trying to shield his love, his sword blocking what it could, but there were so many. Just as he thought it was over, Jimson was there.

“Go!” the dwarf yelled, grabbing Falgrim and hefting her up with a mighty roar, throwing her clear of the group, then kicking Anatarn after her. Jimson smiled and fought the dead, and when they tried to follow after the pair, Jimson reached out and just held them as swords pierced his flesh over and over. “I commend Clan Blackblade,” Jimson said as he fell to both knees, the dead stabbing him again and again. “I commend Clan Blackblade!” A curved sword slid through his throat before he could say it again.

“I’ll kill you all!” Falgrim screamed through her tears as Anatarn picked her up and fell back once more. Of the entire

platoon, there were maybe fifteen dwarves left, and most were in trouble.

Anatarn looked around as the sun started its slow descent and knew they couldn't make their stand here and survive. "Dwarves! To me!" he called out, lifting Falgrim over his shoulder and kicking a skeleton out of the way. The thing wouldn't go down, but a sudden burst of small rocks destroyed it outright.

"I knew you two would still be alive," Eliyan said as she hobbled over to them with two dwarves in tow. The young elf was bloody and exhausted, but still up.

"Good to see you, Eliyan," Anatarn said with a weak smile. He knew that if they could get out of the village, they could at least try to make it further west, into the plains. The dead were slow, and Callen had made no move to finish it yet. Anatarn tightened his grip on Dar'kir and wiped the blood and sweat out of his eyes. Leading the remaining platoon out of the village, he set Falgrim down as they fought a retreating battle west, trying to stay ahead of the dead intent on slaying them all.

"It doesn't look good, does it?" Falgrim asked

"You always look good, now find a weapon and fight...I'm not losing you, too."

"You say the sweetest things," Falgrim said as the dead came at them all.

CHAPTER SIX — HEROES FALL

Queen's Tower, Northern Tsir'illia.

She came awake slowly, as if surfacing from a dark mire that had dragged her down. When she finally opened her eyes, the sunlight was shining in through her windows and illuminating the dust that liked to float around her room. Tolandra Asil tried to sit up, almost passed out, then thought better about trying that again.

"Oh, good, you're awake," a lyrical voice said from across the room. "How do you feel, My Queen?"

Tolandra sighed, knowing that voice. "Like I fell off the cliffs and hit every rock on the way down...then landed on spikes, Ereval," she said as she attempted to at least roll over to see the archmage of Dyln'ir. He was sitting in a woven, high-backed chair with his legs crossed, drinking wine from a large glass. "Thank you again for coming to my rescue, Ereval."

"Well, you gave me quite the fright over the last two days, Tolandra. I almost lost you twice." Ereval stood and walked towards her with a tired smile, setting his wine down and examining her carefully. He pressed on her ribs gently and shook his head, moving his hands to her collarbone and shoulder. "How does this feel?"

"Get to the point where you tell me what I can't do so I can ignore you," Tolandra said, trying to sit up again. She didn't almost pass out this time, but her body felt like she should have. "Amara's leaves, why do I hurt so badly? Did the healing not work?"

Ereval shook his head, his tired smile fading. "It worked, but so many bones were broken, and organs punctured that it took everything I had to keep you alive. The rest will have to be up to your body now."

Tolandra frowned. She knew how healing worked and how much it could repair. Though most wounds—even mortal ones—could be closed and healed, the body could only take so much before shutting down. Healing too much, too fast, and shock would kill you as quickly as the wounds would have. "I have to get up. I'm fairly certain I buried that thing, but it might not stop him."

"I'm not sure..." Whatever Ereval was going to say was lost as a loud bell tolled throughout the tower. That bell—situated at the very top of the Queen's Tower—only meant one thing. Ships were coming towards Tsir'illia. Ereval's face went to a mask of stone as he helped her up, supporting her as they both made their way to her balcony. As they walked out on the balcony, a horn sounded far below.

"I see all the hells are breaking loose on this day, aren't they?" Tolandra said as she shook her head. The horn was the one the general used when warning of advancing troops.

"There," Ereval said, pointing down to the east of the tower.

Tolandra looked and sucked in a silent breath. There in the distance, a lone walker could be seen on the road, a mere speck from this height, yet unmistakable to her as the green glow that accompanied it was known to her. "He's here already? How long was I out?"

"Only two days, My Queen," Ereval answered, his gaze going to the sea now. The elves were scrambling down on the docks, readying their sleek ships to meet the dark specks on the horizon. Ereval clasped both hands together, then tore them apart in a circle motion, revealing a scene between his hands—a close-up of those specks.

"He's here," Tolandra whispered as she saw the five black ships sailing toward her nation. They were the black ships of Raer'drin, the island of Raer'dreth himself. "The Dark War has started, Ereval...and may Amara have mercy on us all.

"Mayhap your niece will have luck with Lorant? They will surely turn the tide if they were to join their ships."

"Possibly, but I haven't heard from her in a very long time, and it would take over a tenday for those ships to get here," Tolandra said as they walked back inside. "I was going to try to message her before the Shadowknight attacked Illren. Rumors on the wind spoke of a massacre in Llor, and I pray that Eliyan is safe."

"You message Eliyan, and I will see if I can visit King Danrae of Branthian. If ships are heading here, it is a safe bet that they are heading for him as well." Ereval bowed and left, already weaving his hands to form the portal to take him to the capital city of Branth.

Tolandra collapsed in a chair and let her arms fall limp. She was in no shape to try battling Samor again, and no one else at the tower would even have half the chance she did. *One thing at a time,* she thought as she sat forward. *Find out how Eliyan is doing, then worry about the dark knight heading for the tower.* Tolandra twisted two fingers in a triangle and sent a message to the general of Tsir'illia.

Fall back and do not face the dark knight head-on. Use delaying tactics and traps only.

When that was done, Tolandra got up and prepared to send a message to Eliyan, then sat back down as her body screamed at her once more. *I have never been so badly beaten in my whole life,* she thought as she winced through the pain. *I'll just rest my eyes and try her in a minute...*

North of Ulant Village, Western Lorant.

The sun was just coming up as the wagon roared out of the western gate of the now-abandoned village of Ulant. The people were heading west toward the Axerun Tower and safety, while Alant, Syn'ella, and their newfound friend Grym rode like the wind for the next village. The militia at the tower was on its way, but would take at least two hours to mobilize, hours these people didn't have. Therefore, Alant rode on with his friends, fighting through the dead and onward.

"There haven't been as many dead as I thought there would be," Syn'ella said as they cleared the village.

"Did ye just curse us, lass?" Grym cried out as the wagon bounced and jostled along the road. The horses were nearing exhaustion, but kept the pace, for now.

Alant laughed as he rode ahead of them, his horse near exhaustion as well. They had pushed their mounts to save the folk of Lorant, but they would have to stop soon, or the beasts would be done for. The young Silverlord looked back at the wagon where Syn'ella was riding and smiled, blowing her a kiss. She wanted to ride with him, but this freed him up to fight better. Alant was about to say something witty when he saw a large gathering up ahead on the plains. Though he couldn't make out exactly what they were, he could guess that they had found the dead. "Stop looking; I found them."

Falgrim stumbled for the hundredth time and swore as she bashed another skeleton with her borrowed hammer. She hated these unwieldy things and missed her axe something fierce. She didn't have any other choice at the moment, however, as they were fighting for their lives by the light of the moon. They had retreated to the western plains from the fallen village of Harvon with fifteen of the platoon; now there were only ten of them left. With the sunset, it was harder to see in the dark, and the dead didn't seem to be hindered by that at all.

"Eliyan, watch the left flank," Anatarn yelled as he parried two curved swords and sliced another skeleton in half.

"Got it," the young elf replied wearily as she sent a burst of rocks at the three dead, trying to move around them. She spun and laid her hands on one of the dwarves that had taken a nasty cut, healing him quickly, but after her spell, she stumbled and fell to both knees.

"To the hells," Falgrim cursed as she limped over and hauled Eliyan to her feet. "Easy on the magic, lass," Falgrim told her in an uncharacteristic show of concern for the elf. Falgrim hated magic, but with Eliyan, she was starting to see that it was just another tool. Just like anything else, though, do something too much, and your body will collapse.

"Can't...only way I can fight," Eliyan replied, tears falling from her violet eyes. She wiped them and gritted her teeth, shaking her head and standing once more as the few soldiers they still had filled in the gap to the left as they kept going west. At least they hoped it was west. It was too dark for landmarks, so they just kept retreating from the dead.

"You're doin' fine, lass. Just stay up," Falgrim said, bashing another dead as it came at them. She was still having a hard time with her ankle, and they were in trouble. Falgrim looked at her love, Anatarn, and marveled at how he was still up and in charge. Dwarves were notoriously tough and could stay on their feet long past most others when it came to exhaustion. By all accounts, this tall human that she had fallen for should be dead on his feet; yet, he was still there, leading them and fighting to keep them safe.

"She comes!" one of the dwarves in the platoon yelled as he took a familiar axe to the shoulder. The weapon had come out of nowhere and slammed into his shoulder, taking him off his feet and sending him into the dead. He was promptly stabbed three times before he could get to his feet, his shouts of defiance rising above the din of battle.

"Me axe!" Falgrim yelled as she saw what hit the dwarf. The dark knight had thrown Falgrim's axe at them. "You'll pay for that, spawn."

The dark knight was striding forward, her sword in hand, as the dead moved aside for her. "Your pointless retreat ends now, human," Callen Drah said, ignoring the dwarf as she advanced. She was heading straight for Anatarn, her fiery eyes blazing. They clashed, sword on sword, and the dark knight was beating Anatarn's sword down with every powerful swing.

Falgrim knew that they were in trouble. Anatarn's sword could hurt that thing, but he was in no shape to take her on. Worse, the dead had moved and were coming at the rest of them from both sides. Falgrim grabbed Eliyan and dragged her towards the fallen dwarf, intent on getting her axe back and helping Anatarn. “Let’s go, girl, this way.”

The dwarf got to one knee, covered in blood and grime, the axe still in his shoulder. “Come on! Is that the best ye got?!”

Falgrim smiled, a sense of pride washing through her. They had lost so many, yet the dwarves wouldn’t give up. “Eliyan, could you heal him without passing out?”

“Don’t worry about me, you just kill everything, and I’ll try to heal him,” the elven wizard said through gritted teeth.

“That’ a girl,” Falgrim rushed in, bashing with her hammer and grabbed the haft of her axe. “This might hurt a wee bit,” she said as she yanked the axe out.

Eliyan was there with both hands as the dwarf screamed in pain, her glowing light pouring into the vicious wound. “I’ve got him,” Eliyan said, but her eyes fluttered, and she fell back, fighting to stay conscious.

Falgrim looked around and felt despair creeping in. Eliyan and the dwarf were down, the other dwarves were slowly being surrounded, and Anatarn was on both knees now, struggling with the dark knight. They were all falling, and she could only help so many. *I knew this was going to be bad,* she thought as she remembered the feeling she had back in Llar. Her own wounds were catching up with her, and she knew this could be the end for them all. Falgrim closed her eyes, praying for the first time since her days in the war. “Gar’heth...show me the way”

“This way!” a tiny voice called to her. “Stand together!”

Falgrim’s eyes snapped open as a small form flew by her, a tiny voice calling out to the dwarves. As soon as the voice said that, a clarion call split the night. A bright light burst out from behind them as the sound of thundering hooves approached.

"Face me, Knight of Shad'ar!" a young man called out, his sword a shining beacon of light as he rode through the left flank, knocking the dead away as he charged on horseback. His silver shield deflected swords as he thundered over the dead; the dwarves were quick to pounce on the fallen, hacking and bashing them before they could rise.

Callen Drah looked up with fiery eyes and backed up slowly, sword at the ready. "Who are you to challenge me?" she said, keeping her eyes on Anatarn as well.

"I am Silverlord Alant Landsir, slayer of Samor Cah," the young man said as he slid off the horse and helped Anatarn to his feet. As the two swords neared each other, a loud hum spread out from them, reverberating through the very air. The two swords seemed like mirror images of each other, one cast in light, the other in darkness.

"Oh, yer screwed now, lassie!" a dwarf called from the approaching wagon. The driver pulled to the right and ran over the dead on that flank, coming around slowly and laughing. The dwarves on that side followed up with the same tactic as the left; pouncing and dismantling the dead as they tumbled down.

Falgrim was stunned speechless, but seeing Anatarn rise broke her out of it, and she spun to help the fallen dwarf. "Up, brave one, we're not out of this yet." She helped him up and looked at Eliyan, her mouth hitting the dirt once again. There, helping Eliyan sit up, was a faerie with long golden hair, golden eyes, and gossamer wings. The tiny thing was only two and a half feet tall and wielded a sword no less. "Who in the cold forge are you?!"

"I'm Syn'ella, Warrior of the Ninth Thorn," the faerie said with pride. The little thing sheathed her sword and flew over, bowing to Falgrim.

"Oh, that explains everything," Falgrim said as Eliyan laughed.

“A faerie, and a Warrior of the Thorn? Your timing is well come, Syn’ella,” Eliyan said, trying to stand.

Falgrim turned to see how the fight was going with Anatarn and the new warrior—and smiled. The dark knight was fighting a purely defensive battle, fending off both skilled swordsmen, and with blades that could harm her. Her armor was rent in two places, and she was backing up, parrying the twin blades in a stance meant to keep them off balance.

Callen Drah spun and slashed out, knocking Anatarn’s blade wide, the tall warrior in black stumbling from exhaustion. Instead of a killing blow, however, Callen turned and made for the wagon that was coming back around, parrying the thrust of the blade of light. As it came, she slashed down and severed the horses from the wagon, leaping onto the back of one and slashing the connecting harness. The dark knight was off into the night before anyone could yell.

“Me horse!” the dwarf called after her, leaping down and rushing to the one that was left.

“Nice sword,” Anatarn said as Alant helped him up while slashing out at a skeleton

“Thanks. Yours is pretty good too,’ Alant said with a weary smile, blocking a curved sword and taking another on his silver shield.

“You two can kiss and cuddle later; we have to finish these dead and get the wounded back to Llar,” Falgrim said, swinging her axe into the dead. It felt so good to have her weapon back.

“They better not cuddle! Alant is mine,” Syn’ella said as she drew her slim sword again, slashing at the wrist of one of the dead as it came at them.

“It was just…, oh, forget it,” Falgrim said with a sigh. She knew better to argue with a faerie, if indeed that was what the little thing truly was. She had only heard stories when she was a wee dwarf, but it seemed like those were coming true before her eyes.

It was hours before they had the dead destroyed and the wounded stabilized. Formal introductions went around as the dwarves helped fix the wagon so they could travel in the morning; the wounded were placed in the back for the night. They traded tales around a fire as they camped; Eliyan was stunned to hear that Alant wielded Ilen'dar.

"Alant, this sword is like the twin of our companion's blade. Ilen'dar and Dar'kir, The Light and the Dark," Eliyan said, almost giddy. "I still don't know the history of Dar'kir, but it has to be entwined with Ilen'dar."

"Again with you elves and naming things. See this? This is me axe. That's it...just me axe. I haven't named it just because I can," Falgrim said as she sat with her arm around Anatarn. He was already asleep, exhaustion taking him as soon as he sat down.

The little faerie completely ignored her and leapt into the air. "I shall name your fine axe, Woundgiver!" Syn'ella said proudly, "or *Wun'lar* in elven."

Falgrim snorted, but a smile played on her lips. It was hard to be grumpy in the face of such, well, light-hearted joy. *How could one tiny body contain that much glee*, she thought. "That would be *R'dar* in dwarven. It means *to rend*."

"I'm just glad that we arrived when we did," Alant said as he sat with Syn'ella. "We're on our way to petition Lorant for aid in the coming war with a dark wizard, and we could use all the heroes we can find."

"I'm not sure how good that will go over," Eliyan said, frowning. "When we fled Llor, that dark knight had slain all the nobles, and the guard funneled us right to her."

"And they didn't even do that well," Falgrim added, stroking Anatarn's brow. She caught herself doing it and snatched her hand back. *This damned bond,* she swore to herself. Yet she could feel it in her heart, and it felt so natural that it made her smile. "But don't worry yerself over it. We'll get ye there, and you can try talking to the king." Falgrim wasn't so sure that it would go well, but there was something about this young man that told her he could do the impossible.

Ruins of the Lonely Tower, Endless Wastes

His feet shuffled through the sand as he searched for the buried entrance, the harsh winds driving sand into his squinted eyes relentlessly. Raer'dreth frowned as, once again, he failed to find the way into the sunken tower that he had remembered from centuries past. The archmage had arrived over a day ago via his magic and stepped into one of the worst sandstorms he had ever encountered. His magic was keeping him relatively safe, yet he couldn't find the way in. He stopped and shook his head, his long white hair caked with sand. He crooked his hands again in a sweeping motion and gritted his teeth as the sand around the base of the buried tower shifted away, his magic digging furrows away from the ancient stone walls.

It has to be here, he thought as he swept his hands again, dredging up another great swath of sand. The soft, unforgiving particles just flowed right back in from the sides, hindering his progress. Raer'dreth recalled that the door was on the southern face of the tower and, even though the sun was obscured by the storm, he knew he was in the right location. *It must be deeper than I anticipated.*

He dropped his hands and swirled three fingers in a figure eight, calling upon his magic to cleanse the sand from him once more, giving him a minute of freedom from the onslaught of the relentless storm. The archmage wasn't used to failing in anything and hadn't been this frustrated in a very long time. He took a second to clear his mind and focus, taking a deep breath while the limited magic kept the sand from his face. Then it hit him...the storm wasn't natural! Grinning, Raer'dreth brought both hands around in front of him and entwined his fingers, snapping them taut and sending his magic out in a wave. The dispelling force met some resistance, but shattered the sandstorm, breaking the ward and scattering the winds. Within moments, the sky was clear and the sun shone down on the barren landscape. Raer'dreth smiled and saw that the top of the door was indeed near where he had been digging—only a foot off to the side. He cleared the rest of the sand with magic and made a path down to the solid, ancient door, opening it with his spells, and holding his breath as the sealed, musty air escaped like a whistling wind.

No one has been in this tower in over two centuries, he thought as he lit a faded torch on the wall with a snap of his fingers. The archmage walked in carefully but confidently, finding the main antechamber and staring in wonder; it was like stepping back in time. The floor was covered in an inch of dust, but the stone chairs and tables still stood where they had been, ceramic plates and cups left as they were. This tower had been the center of the mighty kingdom of Jal'rien and was situated in the city of Anor. Now called the Lonely Tower by explorers from the nearby G'lar oasis, Raer'dreth knew that the place was much more than a ruined tower. This place was the seat of the Jal'rien mages; within these stone walls, the archmage of shadow would once again unleash destruction upon his enemies.

This time, I will lay waste to all of Alian'tir, he thought as he searched for what he needed to amplify his spell. Raer'dreth was powerful, but for the spell he was casting to affect the entire continent, he would need to boost his magic even more. Footfalls behind him caused him to spin and unleash a blast of fire from his fingertips, only to wash over the figure harmlessly.

"Master? What are you doing *here*?" Callen Drah asked incredulously as she wiped both sand and ash from her armor.

"Callen? How did you come to be in the middle of the Endless Wastes?" Raer'dreth asked, ignoring her question. "I commanded you to lead the dead into Lorant."

Callen folded her arms over her chest, glaring at him with those flaming eyes. "I was routed by that cursed blade, Dar'kir, as well as another blade, this one shining like the sun," she admitted, hanging her head in shame. "As I fled into the wastes, I saw the storm and knew some power was here. It called to me, so I came seeking what mysterious power was stirring."

Raer'dreth smiled and patted her on the shoulder. "Well, you are well come, loyal servant." He turned and strode off, beckoning her to follow. "Now that you are here, you can help me look for the library. I have a new mission for you."

Capital City of Llor, Nation of Lorant

She held on as the wagon bounced and rocked over the rough road, her tailbone bruised from the harsh ride, even on these expensive pillows and blankets. Eliyan Safril, niece to the

Queen of Tsir'illia and wizard-healer, had seen a lot more than she ever thought she would when she had left her home all those days ago. It was supposed to be a simple political meeting that turned into a life-or-death battle. She had learned a lot about herself—her limits and strengths—since then and had proven herself in battle. The young elf had never fought before in a real fight, and now she had survived three, rather harrowing, encounters with death; this last one was the closest so far.

Eliyan brushed her white hair out of her violet eyes and looked out of the back of the covered wagon. They had made it back to the city of Llar with the fallen dwarves and told them about the battle with the dead as well as Alant's quest. The Mayor of Llar had pledged his support right there without bothering to contact the king, sending Belsa Harlow—the new commander of Llar's forces since the fall of Jimson—with an entire dwarven regiment to Branthian right away. Alant had asked Grym to accompany her and penned a missive for the dwarven writer to present to the Knight-Commander of Fort Yarin, allowing them passage in the name of the Silverlord. Now, nearly three days later, Eliyan and her friends were heading into Llor, yet she couldn't help but wonder if Ongril and the rest of her retinue had stayed safe.

"Are you alright, Eliyan?" Syn'ella asked, flying over to the young elf in the wagon.

"I'm just worried about my servants and our fate," Eliyan confessed. She found solace in the tiny faerie's company, feeling at home for the first time since she had left Tsir'illia. The faerie and Eliyan were riding in the back of the wagon while Falgrim, Alant, and Anatarn rode beside it. They expected trouble and wanted a quick getaway in case it all went south. They had all talked the whole way, and Eliyan was stunned to hear about the soulbond between the faerie and the human.

"I'm sure your people stayed hidden and out of sight," Syn'ella assured her with a smile.

Eliyan felt the wagon slow to a halt and heard Alant and Falgrim speaking to someone. Before she could ask Syn'ella to go find out what was going on, Falgrim was at the back of the wagon.

"Looks like we are just in time for a public execution," the female dwarf said with a wry smile.

"It's not Ongril, is it?" Eliyan asked, her heart dropping.

"No. Surprisingly, it's King Albron who will be losing his head this day," Falgrim said with a chortle. "And no, I've no idea what happened. Just sit tight until we can see how safe it is in there."

"Don't worry, Eliyan, I will protect you," Syn'ella said with a small pat on the elf's shoulder.

"I know you will, Brave Syn'ella." Eliyan smiled, knowing that she could protect herself now as well. *I can see High Wizard Jaren's face now when I get home and show him how much I've learned*, she thought. Jaren Highleaf was the High Wizard of Ulin'or and was in charge of training the royal House Safril. He always told her that she had it in her to be better, and now she would show him...If they made it through whatever else was going to come crashing down on them.

The noise of the city crashed around them as the wagon cleared the gate, and Eliyan could see the people out the back as they travelled down the cobblestone road. There was cheering and people with banners, as well as children scurrying by with packages. It didn't look like the dark, gloomy city they had first seen.

"I love festivals," Syn'ella said as she looked out of the wagon. "Everyone seems so happy. Was the king that bad?"

"I never got to meet him," Eliyan said. "We were ambushed rather quickly and had to flee south." The sound of talking drew her attention, and she could hear Falgrim laughing.

Eliyan jumped when the guards came around the back of the wagon, yet tears sprang to her eyes when she heard a familiar voice.

"Milady, please come out of that filthy wagon and give me a hug," Ongril said, stepping from behind the guards.

Eliyan climbed out, hugging her trusted servant. "Oh, Ongril, I was worried about you all. Have you stayed safe?"

"Indeed, and it is quite the story to tell, but now we must get you all to the ceremony. I can't be late," Ongril said with a smirk. "Though it pleases me that you are safe, milady."

"You should've seen her fight, Ongril. Your *lady* did alright on the field of battle," Falgrim said, slapping him on the shoulder.

"Coming from a dwarf, that is high praise indeed," Ongril said with a weak smile as he rubbed his shoulder. He motioned to the guards, and they led the way through the streets as Ongril walked with Eliyan.

Eliyan looked around her in wonder at the human city, really seeing it for the first time, since the last time she was here, it was all a blur. The buildings were well-made, mostly out of stone with some lumber, and the smoke from the hearths drifted out of stone chimneys all around the city. Soon, they arrived at the massive stone square where the company fought Callen Drah. Gone were the blood-soaked stones and the dozens of bodies, replaced with a stage upon which stood Albron in chains, waiting to lose his head. The man's eyes looked to have been burned away, and he was almost feral as he fought his bonds.

The company stood in silence as the charges were read aloud to the citizens of Lorant. Cheers went up as the story of Alsan's and Ongril's heroic deeds was spoken. They all watched as the headsman carried out the sentence, the former king's head falling from his body with cheers from the crowd. It wasn't a bloodthirsty cry, however. It was more of a cry for freedom. The dark times were over, or so said the general of Lorant's army, as the body was carried away. The crowd started to disperse as a woman came over to them.

"You can't know how relieved I am to finally meet you all," the woman said. She was a little over five feet tall and thin, her hips flaring out in all the right places. She had deep brown eyes and long brown hair, with two braids on the sides. The woman had a rugged jaw line and broad shoulders, seeming more handsome than beautiful.

"Lady Eliyan Safril, I introduce you to the Soon-to-be Queen of Lorant, Alsan Brenshin," Ongril said, bowing to both women.

"I never heard ol' Alban had himself a daughter," Falgrim said, as she eyed the woman up and down.

"I was a hidden, dirty secret. Nevertheless, I could not sit by while my brother conspired with the growing darkness descending on our lands," Alsan said as she smiled at Ongril. "In the coming days, old records will be unsealed, and my birth will be known to all the citizens of Lorant." Alsan stepped a little closer to Ongril, looking at him again.

"Oh, my axe, you're smitten with him, aren't ye?" Falgrim said, looking from Alsan to Ongril and back again.

Eliyan laughed out loud at the face Alsan made, going to the woman's side quickly. "My Queen, ignore the fair dwarf. She has her courtship to worry about," Eliyan said, pointing to Anatarn as Falgrim turned red in the face, looking down at her feet.

"You taught her too well, Falgrim," Anatarn said, laughing. The big warrior wrapped his arm around the dwarf and kissed her head.

“Why don’t we all head to the palace and talk?” Ongril suggested. “I think the stories we all have to share may need a good drink, or five. It will be a good diversion until Alsan is crowned Queen tomorrow night. Until then, we can play catch-up and figure out what we can all do.

“You always know exactly what to say and do, Ongril. That is why you are going to be my personal advisor,” Alsan said, smiling at him. “If the Lady Safril will part with you, that is?”

“Of course, whatever makes my dear friend happy.” Eliyan was smiling, yet a feeling in her gut said something was coming; something terrible. She tried to put on a happy face—after all, her trusted servants were alive and, it seemed, her steward was a hero. In the back of her mind, though, she feared it was all for nothing.

CHAPTER SEVEN — DARK DAYS

Capital City of Branth, Nation of Branthian

The woman stood at the ship's bow as the salty winds sent her long black hair out behind her like a banner. Hylana Brendal had a knot in the pit of her stomach, and it had only gotten worse after leaving the port of Branth. She wore her white robes tied at the waist by a silver cord with her amethyst stone hung from her neck on a silver chain. The cord signified her recent promotion to High Sorceress, second only to Gerick Eldon, who stayed back at the castle with the rest of the sorcerers and protected the king.

Hylana was second in command of the fleet, answering only to Knight General Marveth, who was promoted to the head of the Branthian fleet after surviving the waves of the dead out of the Endless Wastes. They had set sail with eight fully crewed ships, as well as over twenty Branthian sorcerers. Hylana closed her eyes and tried to calm her nerves, yet the distant black ships made that impossible. There were said to be only seven black ships...but something felt wrong.

"Shard for your thoughts?" a melodic voice asked from behind her.

Hylana smiled and opened her eyes, still amazed that this elf treated her as an equal. "The same thoughts I voiced before we left—that sailing towards a small fleet of religious fanatics bent on our demise is not a great idea."

Ereval Drial came up beside her and rested one foot on the guide ropes of the ship, staring out at the incoming ships. The Archmage of Dyln'ir had his usual flowing white hair tied up with a small leather cord as his piercing violet eyes scanned the horizon. He was dressed in white silk trimmed with gold, with a silver sash tied at the waist. He had arrived in the court of Branth to tell them of the black ships, just as the warnings sounded. When he heard that the nation of Branth was sailing to meet them, he decided to stay and help.

"I still echo those doubts, dear lady, yet the king seems sure that this will be an easy victory." Ereval turned to her, smiling, and laid his slender hand on her shoulder. "Now, let us go and find the others and get ready for this little attack." The elven archmage turned to go, but her hand held his arm fast.

"Why are you here, Ereval?"

"I told you. I sail with you to assist Branth against the dark ships," Ereval began slowly as he looked down at her hand on his arm. "This is a war, Hylana. Not only against Tsir'illia, but against all of Alian'tir."

"I'm aware of that. I was there when you gave that pretty speech to the court right after you walked out of a portal—which again, bypassed all the wards we have set up—but why would you help us when you told us that the dark ships also sail towards your lands?"

Ereval's gaze softened and turned to one of mirth. "Those wards were changed after Alant united our two nations, but to answer your question more directly...I'm curious."

"Curious?" Hylana could hear the commands of the sorcerers now, readying the crew for a spell battle as the dark ships sailed closer. "What could an all-powerful elf be curious about regarding us mere humans?" she asked with a playful smile.

"Elves command magic with an inherited grace and skill. All we need is to form the right gestures, and we cause the magic to do our whim." Ereval undid his hair and let the long white locks fall free in the wind. "But you sorcerers...you found a way to cast magic despite all our warnings and threats. You use those little stones and speak your blasphemous words..."

Hylana's eyes widened in shock at his words. She had studied the ancient ways of how humans gained their magic—ancient pacts with dark powers to learn forbidden words of power—but nothing in their texts or tomes mentioned being warned away or threatened by the elves for delving into it. It was common knowledge that the elves disliked their ways, but this was new to her.

"Don't look so shocked, I'm sure your histories would've erased that bit of knowledge. It was not a time that some of us are proud of." Ereval stretched his fingers and loosened up his arms as the Branthian ships started moving into formation. The ships spread out from each other as the Branthian sorcerers lined the decks. "So, yes. I am curious to see firsthand how you sneaky little sorcerers use this forbidden magic and to study you up close." The archmage winked at her and walked towards the other sorcerers as they lined up, just as Knight General Marveth came over to her.

"Don't say it, I know," the general said, holding up a hand in surrender. Sarin Marveth had short grey hair and deep brown eyes; his old plate armor replaced by sturdy sailing leathers. He had been Knight-Captain in Fort Kaldrin— also known as Knight's Rest in Branthian—when she had met him with Alant. "You think this is a bad idea."

Hylana smiled and shook her head. "Yes, but I know we have to try. I just have a bad feeling about this. It's too easy and very cliché of the enemy to sail against a larger fleet without something up their sleeve."

"That's why we have over twenty sorcerers along with us, Hylana. Anything they throw at us, you can counter and retaliate before we even start firing cannons." Knight General Marveth turned and blew a horn he took from his belt, signaling the ships to go ahead full speed. The Branthian ships were lighter and faster than the bigger black ships, and they could maneuver better.

Hylana saw his brow furrow, her stomach twisting in knots. "What is it?"

"They aren't breaking formation. We're moving to flank them, and they aren't bothering to care. All seven ships are still coming straight at us." Marveth shared a look with Hylana before glowing darts of magic came arcing across the skies at them from the black ships. "Why aren't they attacking the ships directly?" he asked as the lead sorcerers threw up their magic wards and died screaming as the magic tore through them as if the shields weren't there.

"Because they are taking out your advantage first, general!" Ereval called out as he ran over. The elf made a fist, summoning a strong wind that knocked both Hylana and Marveth a good ten feet away, just as spears of acid slammed into the deck where they had been standing.

"How?" Hylana called out as she stood and grabbed her stone. Before she could say the word of power for her warding shield, Ereval stopped her and pointed to the lead black ship. She could see a figure holding a sword and slicing himself across his hand, and her stomach clenched in dread.

"They have bloodmages," Ereval said in a grave tone. "Our wards will be useless, even mine."

Hylana knew then that her gut had been right—this was a trap all along. “How did our magic not sense them?” she asked, knowing that the answer was pointless. Bloodmages were human sorcerers who went even darker for the magic they craved. They used stones and words as well, but amplified the spells with blood as a catalyst to allow their spells to bypass wards and even armor, as it targeted the very lifeblood of the enemy directly.

“I don’t know,” the elven archmage answered, “but it appears we are losing sorcerers quickly. If the enemy takes out enough of them....” Ereval left the rest unsaid as he spun, using his magic to save another sorcerer.

Hylana held her amethyst and said a word of power. “Wirin!” The wind spun around her, picking up crates and using them as makeshift shields. Bloodmagic could ignore magic wards and sometimes armor, but normal things could still give some cover. The crates deflected some of an incoming ice spell, but she took cuts across her back and arms as the magic came through. She knew they were caught in a trap and had to break free. “We have to turn around,” the sorceress said as she lifted a crate and blocked a stream of fire heading for another sorcerer.

Marveth stood and nodded. “That’s why they didn’t care about the flanking ships; those ships will never get close enough to matter.”

“None of us will,” Ereval continued. His eyes turned to the north, and tears rolled down his pale face. “Not even the elves.”

“I’m sure they are doing fine, Ereval. The elves are better at magic after all, right?” Hylana said, trying to comfort him. If bloodmages were attacking Tsir’illia, they would be in trouble as well.

Knight General Marveth put the horn to his lips, but before he could sound the retreat, a blast of fire slammed into him and sent his body tumbling into the cabin behind.

Hylana dove for cover and grasped her stone. "Wirial," she intoned, saying the word of power, and grabbing the horn with the very wind around them. She pulled the horn to her and cooled it, then sounded the retreat, praying that they could make it back to warn everyone.

Marveth rolled and tried to stand, as four spears of acid pinned him down, screaming. Water splashed over his form as Ereval flicked his fingers towards the Knight General, yet it was too late.

"You're in charge now," Ereval said as the ships turned sharply.

"I know, but I wish I weren't." Hylana watched as one, then another of the Branthian ships caught fire, their dying sorcerers unable to stop the magic from consuming them. Without spells to protect the ships, those bloodmages could just sink the vessels before they could return fire. Some of the ships were firing anyway, desperate actions in the face of certain doom, but the shots fell short before the magic consumed them too.

Hylana turned to the crew and surviving sorcerers that had hastily spun the ship, their fear etched on their rugged faces. "Use your magic to send messages to the others who survive. Tell them to use wind to fill the sails and get us ahead of those spells." They nodded and got to it. She slumped down and closed her eyes, tears for the fallen general falling slowly down her face.

"You did very well," Ereval said as they gained some distance from the pursuing black ships. "I've never seen your magic up close, and I have to say you adapted well to the threat."

"High praise indeed from an elven wizard," Hylana said with a slight smile as she covered Marveth's body. "Thank you for helping, Ereval. Now let's get back and warn everyone. This war is going to be bad."

Capital City of Llor, Nation of Lorant

She smiled as the queen talked, trying to pay attention but failing miserably. Eliyan Safril was far from the healer she started as, and even now, she traced the scar on her arm from her recent battles.

"Eliyan?"

"Yes, I'm sorry. What did you say, Queen Alsan?"

"I said, you seem troubled this morning, Eliyan...and it's just Alsan when we are alone." Alsan smiled and walked over. "It's been a day and a half since you all arrived, and you still look like you're running from something.

The elven healer looked away and frowned. She couldn't possibly tell the woman that she had a nightmare about her. Her dream last night was dark, and she hadn't had one of those since she was very young. Most of it had fled with the dawn, yet she could still see Alsan leaning over her, a look of pure fear on the woman's face. Whatever was going to happen to the queen, Eliyan feared it would be her fault.

"I'm just nervous about the entire war, Alsan. Even with our three nations united, the dark forces are still a threat."

"You're worried about your queen still?" Alsan asked as she sat on the bed and leaned back. They had been spending a lot of time together since the coronation, mainly because Alsan truly didn't have any friends or family left.

"I haven't heard from her at all. Never before have I not heard from her when I travel, especially when I'm doing so in her name."

"Have you tried sending her a message?" Alsan patted the bed and motioned for Eliyan to sit.

"I tried right before the coronation, but I didn't get an answer." Eliyan's eyes closed as she sat next to the woman on the bed, her shoulders sagging as she started to cry. "I should've sent something before, but with all the fighting and..."

Alsan's strong arm encircled the lithe elf and pulled her close. "It's alright. Let it out. I'm sure everything is fine."

Eliyan was going to thank the newly crowned queen of Lorant when her head throbbed with power. She cried out as magic burst into her skull, Queen Tolandra's voice booming in her mind.

Eliyan! Do not come home. Dark ships have destroyed our fleet, and a Shadowknight approaches the tower. I fear I cannot fight the dark knight much longer; my magic is almost useless against the creature. Flee, dear girl, and remember me!

Eliyan cried out again, this time in grief and fear. "No. My Queen!"

"Guards!" Alsan called loudly, raising the alarm. "Eliyan, what is it. What assails you?" Alsan held her close, supporting her as she stood.

"Queen Tolandra is in grave danger. I must get home now."

Alant burst in with the guards, the rest of the company right on his heels. "What is it, Eliyan?" the young Silverlord asked, concern written on his face.

"It's Queen Tolandra...a Shadowknight is attacking her tower in Tsir'illia along with dark ships. I have to go to her."

"And how are we going to do that?" Falgrim asked as she brandished her axe. "It would take far too long to get there if they are in trouble now, even with the sleek Lorant ships."

"I...I..." Eliyan stopped and took a deep breath, trying to calm herself. *Tolandra needs me, and I am not a helpless little girl anymore. Think...think.*

"Can you send me there?" Alant asked, determination set in his stern visage. "I slew a Shadowknight once, and I'm more than ready to do it again."

"Yes! I know magic can transport you places, but could you send someone else, Eliyan?" The little faerie asked as she flew in circles around Eliyan's head, clearly worried.

Eliyan turned her head and smiled. She knew what she needed to do. It would take everything she had, but she would do it to save her queen; she would do anything to save Tolandra. "Yes, but I fear she will need all of you. Quickly, gather your gear and meet me in the throne room." Eliyan turned to Alsan and laid a slender hand on the woman's broad shoulder. "Can you seal the courtroom and make sure Ongril is somewhere else?"

Alsan looked worried but nodded, her tone serious. "I can, but you need to tell me why."

"Because what I'm going to do is very dangerous and I fear he will try to stop me," Eliyan said bluntly. "I don't want that on him."

"You're going to get me in trouble with him, aren't you?" Alsan asked with a wry grin. "Tell me that it isn't too dangerous..."

"It's not," Eliyan lied as they rushed to the queen's throne room. Eliyan heard the Queen of Lorant issue orders to clear the court and to send Ongril a message to meet her in the stables. The elven healer tried to recall her mentor's teachings about portals and closed her eyes, hearing his voice as he paced around her desk. Eliyan lost herself in the memory, focusing on his words and blocking everything else out.

"Opening a doorway, or portal, to somewhere else is relatively easy, stepping through instantaneously to where you want to go. All you need is a clear picture in your mind of where you're going," Jaren Highleaf said in his lecturing tone. "Sending someone else is a little harder, especially if you aren't going with them." The High Wizard of Ulin'or smiled down at her and bent down closer. "You would need a lot of power to hold the portal open to make sure they arrive before shutting it. You might cut them in half if it shut too quickly. Struggling against the very weft of the world is hard, even for two seconds."

Eliyan snapped out of her memory and frowned. She needed to hold this portal open for a very long time…long enough to send all of her friends through. That would require the magic of at least three archmages...or maybe not. *I've only read about life magic, but I'm going to have to try.*

Life magic was the opposite of blood magic, using the caster's very life essence to fuel their spells. It was only in the ancient texts as a last stand type of thing, as the caster always died to fuel their magic to the heights of legend.

"Alright, we're all here," Alant said as they entered the throne room. He was standing tall like his title suggested, with Syn'ella right there next to him.

"Now, what can we do, Eliyan?" Anatarn said as he stood there with his sword out and his smile wide. Falgrim was next to him, her death's head grin no longer frightening the elven healer.

Eliyan looked at her friends with a smile. She would miss them, yet they were the queen's only hope. "Just come closer," Eliyan said as she took a steadying breath. "I'm going to open a portal, just outside the Queen's Tower, and you all are going through. Save her and anyone else you can."

"Isn't that going to wear you out casting so many portals?" Syn'ella asked, worry creasing her tiny brow.

"It would. That is why I'm only opening one. I will hold it open as long as I can for all of you." Eliyan thanked Amara that no one in this room knew what that would entail... Two seconds for one person would certainly drain her. She would need to hold the portal open for almost five or six seconds for them all. It would take her entire essence to keep it open and steady. This is the reason she didn't want Ongril here. He would know and stop her.

"Are you sure, Eliyan?" Alant asked.

"Yes. Now be ready, and may you all be safe." Eliyan caught Falgrim's eyes, her gaze softening. "Give them hell for me, Falgrim." Before the dwarf could retort, she wove her hands in the intricate gestures of the spell to open a portal, picturing the green grass of the tower that she idolized as a child. The very stones and gardens around it came to life in her mind as the magic snapped open the glowing disc in front of her. "Now...go!"

The companions filed through one at a time as quickly as they could, but she could already feel the magic fading. She twisted her pinky in a slow circle and channeled her very life into the magic, steadying it and rooting herself as the doorway. She wished that she could have thanked them for what they had taught her, to be strong and stand tall. She owed them so much for everything; at least, she would make her life count for something. *I hope Falgrim will be proud of me*, she thought as her body trembled under the weight of the very weft of the world. She was at four seconds, and she could feel her life slipping away.

As if the dwarf could hear her, Falgrim stopped and smiled back. "I'm proud of ye, girl." Then stepped through.

Five seconds. *Almost....*

"Eliyan? What's wrong?" Alsan asked from what seemed like very far away. "Eliyan!"

Six. *Where am I?*

Eliyan closed her eyes and felt the cold stone floor on her back. *Why can I feel that on my back?* The elven healer opened her eyes and saw Alsan over her, the woman's face etched in horror as Eliyan felt herself fading away. She held up a hand, which was almost transparent, and felt the portal snap closed with an audible snap that echoed through the entire world...or so she thought. *I did it...I sent them all through. I truly am a wizard...*

"Eliyan...hold on. Do you hear me?" Alsan's voice was getting louder and more solid. "Damn this girl to the hells. Well, at least no one else is here. I don't know what I'm doing, so hold on."

Eliyan felt a warm tingling spread across her face and neck, travelling down her whole body. She wasn't floating anymore, and she could feel something spreading through her very nerves, coiling around her heart and lungs and travelling out into her arms, legs, and neck...*pain!*

"Ah!" Eliyan cried out as the pain shot through her entire being, making her scream almost endlessly. Her throat seemed raw, and she thrashed on the stone floor, something lifting her again.

Alsan's voice sounded lighter, like she was exhausted. "It's alright, you're back. Hold on to me now...just breathe." Alsan lifted her as more people screamed her name.

Eliyan opened her eyes to a soft, blue haze. Alsan's hands were glowing with magic. "What...how?" She could feel the woman everywhere around her, surrounding her, pouring into her, stabilizing her. Everything was going dark again, but not as transparent.

"Eliyan!"

Eliyan could hear Ongril's panicked voice as he came closer.

"It's alright, Ongril. I have her." Alsan said as the glow faded. "She is back, but she needs to rest...I think I need to rest as well. "

A loud thud followed Alsan's words, and Eliyan felt herself hit the floor again, painfully this time. That was all Eliyan knew before the enveloping darkness finally claimed her. *I'm coming home, Mother...*

Ruins of the Lonely Tower, Endless Wastes

The archmage looked down at the stone dais and smiled; everything was ready for his retribution, and the twins were preparing to transfer the soulgems here for Raer'dreth. With those here, Raer'dreth could animate the souls of his Knights of Shad'ar as they fell, keeping the fight going against Branthian and Tsir'illia simultaneously. As long as they weren't slain too quickly, he could keep a steady flow of souls and not tire too much.

The archmage took a deep breath and swirled his fingers in an intricate pattern that he had only done once before in his very long life. Back then, it was a hasty spell, cast to impress his fellow wizards and end the war, showing off his newly gained powers from the dark goddess. Now, however, the dark archmage was more prepared and had taken the time to fuel the spell, making it travel further with a nexus crystal that had been the Jal'rien mages' pride and joy. He could hear the howling winds pick up outside the buried temple and feel the dark magic solidify with the storm and grow.

"Master..." Callen Drah started, but she stopped talking at the withering look he shot her.

When he was done, Raer'dreth slumped back against the wall and smiled weakly. "It is done. The storm now forms and will be on its way to Branthian, killing everything in its wake." Raer'dreth turned to the Knight of Shad'ar. "I want you to follow the storm, riding its heels with the dead and into Branthian. Kill everything that eludes the dark storm." He walked away from his loyal knight and grabbed a bottle of wine he had conjured. He didn't bother to watch her depart— she had to follow his commands, even if she didn't like it.

Now they will all pay, he thought, leaning on the wall for support. The spell took a lot out of him, but he would be fine in an hour or so. *Then I will watch the destruction from afar and rejoice.*

CHAPTER EIGHT — DECISIONS MADE

Fields Outside of Folris, Southern Branthian.

She stomped through the tents and smiled at her troops as they set camp; they had come a long way at a very hard pace, but now they could rest up before the final push. Belsa Harlow walked towards the main gate of Folris with her head held high and a hand on her axe, her long blond hair now in warrior braids. A guard walking out of the town hailed her, and she couldn't help but smirk. Alant had told her of a certain lieutenant, and the description fit this man perfectly, scar and all. "Lieutenant Haves?"

"Yes, I am, and you must be Commander Harlow of Llar," Lieutenant Haves replied, smiling widely as he bowed before her. The man had a strange look on his face and kept staring at her in awe.

"What? Never seen a dwarf afore?"

"Yes, I have," Haves replied. "What I have *never* seen is the distance you all have covered in only four days. I didn't believe it when I got the Knight-Commander 's message this morning, so I had to come see for myself."

"Well, I wouldn't want to do it again, let me tell ya," Belsa said with a laugh. "Dwarves are hardy, but even we have our limits. Thankfully, a patrol boat from the fort met us on the lake and read our missive, letting us sail straight here."

"It's true then? Lorant and Branthian have a truce?"

"Of a sort. There is a dark war coming, and we will stand with ye against it. Now, I heard you don't mind feedin' a bunch of dwarves?" Belsa looked the lieutenant up and down and had to respect the man. He stood like a warrior, and that scar was impressive.

"Food is already being gathered up for twenty dwarves," Haves said with a nod. "And, as a bonus, ten guardsmen and I will be marching with you in the morning to Branth."

"Aye, that is good to hear. It should take us a good two days to get there..." Belsa would have said more, but a horn sounded, snapping her head around as she drew her axe.

"What is it?" Lieutenant Haves asked, drawing his sword as well.

"That's our guide, Grym. Something approaches the camp. Come, Lieutenant, let us see what wants to taste our steel this day." Belsa sprinted to the other side of the camp just as a small force of mounted knights rode up and reigned in. At their head was a fat man in ornate armor, a pretty sword in his plump hand.

"Lord Noro? What are you doing here with a mounted force?" Lieutenant Haves asked, relaxing a bit.

"I am here to conscript your men, Lieutenant," the lord scowled. "You will ride with me back to Oliar and join my forces." The plump lord looked out at the gathering of tents and smiled, turning to a man with the markings of a Knight-Captain. "Knight-Captain Coran. Bring these dwarves as well; they could be useful."

Belsa started forward, a death grip on her axe, but was stopped by Haves as he stepped in front of her. She could see that most of the mounted warriors looked uncomfortable, and one man in particular—this Knight-Captain Coran—seemed almost disgusted. The man had piercing green eyes and long black hair, with a huge sword on his back.

"What is the danger, My Lord?" The Lieutenant asked as he eyed the mounted knights. "To conscript a neighboring town would require a wartime writ from King Danrae himself. I assume you have one?"

Grym came up and stood by Belsa, his eyes troubled. "The men are ready, Belsa," he whispered as the exchange kept going between the Branthians.

Lord Noro bristled. "You *will* come with me, *Lieutenant*, or my men will bring you in for sedition. The king has lost the faith of the people by allying with the disgusting faerie folk. I will rule Branthian after he is thrown down."

Belsa patted Grym on the shoulder—the sign to fall back and get ready for a fight—and stomped towards the lord, pushing Haves out of the way. "Let me see if I got this straight," she began, eyeing the other men as she spoke. "You are against the King of Branthian and want to conscript the dwarves to your cause to overthrow him?"

"Yes. Now listen here, dwarf, I..." Lord Noro would have said more, but Belsa's axe flew through the air and slammed into his chest with such force that he was unhorsed, falling into the grass as he gasped his last breath, his hands feebly clawing the grass around him as he faded.

"Hold!" Lieutenant Haves called out as over half of the knights drew steel. He drew his blade and backed up, seeing dwarves pour in behind him, weapons ready, with Grym at their head, a slender handled axe in his steady hand.

Belsa looked right at Knight-Captain Coran among the mounted knights and smiled. "You. I have a missive declaring this company of dwarves an ally to King Danrae of Branthian. As such, I just put down a revolt. You are welcome." She eyed the man as she walked to the fallen lord and yanked her axe free, wiping it on the robes of the plump corpse. The gathered knights all squirmed in their saddles, looking to the Knight-Captain.

"Is this true, Lieutenant Haves?" Knight-Captain Coran asked as he slid cautiously off his horse.

"Yes, Knight-Captain. Silverlord Alant signed it himself," Lieutenant Haves said with a sigh of relief. "I am heading to Branth with a squad of guards to assist these good dwarves."

"Very well." The Knight-Captain turned to three men. "Faves, Arn, and Heln. Ride back to Oliar and inform Lady Nara that she is in temporary command until King Danrae can be informed. I will ride with these good dwarves with the rest of the company and inform the king in person." The big knight smiled at Belsa and offered his hand. "I am Cassias Coran, Knight-Captain of Oliar. You, milady, have a very good arm there."

"Ha! Thank you, good knight," Belsa said with a roaring laugh. "Now, how about we all eat and discuss our journey on the morrow to Branth?"

Queen's Gardens, Northern Tsir'illia.

He stepped out of the magical portal and felt sick. Disorientation made his head spin, and he almost lost his wide-brimmed hat. Anatarn Blackblade drew Dar'kir out of habit and steadied himself as the sounds of battle came to his trained ears.

"Anatarn, are you alright?" Alant called out as he drew his sword, Ilen'dar. The two swords hummed as they sensed each other, and the warriors had to smile.

"Yeah, just dizzy from the magic. Where is Falgrim?" Anatarn looked around and saw that they had appeared in a garden of beautiful flowers and hedges, with high trellises of vines acting as arches leading out. Steel clashing with steel and the screams of the dying echoed in the salt air, with occasional thunderous explosions that must be from cannon fire.

"Here, Anatarn!" Falgrim called as she kicked a dark knight in the gut and brought her axe down on his helm. "More dark knights, but these aren't as bad as the woman, at least." As soon as she said that, the dark knight skillfully came at her and had her backpedaling.

Syn'ella flew around them and screamed. "This way, quick!" and off she went through the northern trellis.

Anatarn followed Alant, and together they slammed into a force of warriors—barbaric fighters dressed in dark furs with wide eyes and holy symbols wrapped around their weapons. They were everywhere, chanting Raer'dreth's name as they fought. They seemed consumed with fury, and with dark knights supporting them with their swords of ash and mages calling forth lashes of red lightning, it did not look good.

"Alant, the Queen should be up in that tower. She needs help!" Syn'ella called as she flew around and stabbed a warrior with her slim sword.

Anatarn saw elves in groups, fighting back as their smoking ships lay beached upon the shores. Wide-eyed warriors poured out of the black boats onto the docks, and mages stood tall, blasting elves with magic that seemed to go right through their wards. "Bloodmages," Anatarn spat.

"Aye, and we both know how to handle them, don't we, Love?" Falgrim said, winking at him as she finally dropped the dark knight. The dwarf lowered her shoulder and plowed through the ranks of fighters, barreling toward the mages before they could see her.

"Syn'ella, follow her, I'll be right behind you," Anatarn said, dispatching two warriors with his black blade and kicking a third out of Alant's flank. He could feel Dar'kir hum in response to Alant's sword. It seemed that if they were close, the two swords became more powerful. "Alant, get up there and save the queen."

"Oh, thank the Gods someone else is in charge," Alant said as he shield-bashed past two warriors. "I was getting tired of doing it all the time." He brought his sword down on a dark knight's shield arm, spun, then stabbed the knight as light flared brightly, eliciting a horrid scream from the undead knight as its soul fled.

Anatarn laughed at the light-hearted quip and focused on catching up to his love. He still couldn't believe that he had fallen for Falgrim so quickly, yet she had his heart as solidly as she held that axe. *It has to be a Heartbond, but why hasn't she said anything?* he thought, trying not to get too distracted. He didn't want to press it, but...

"You there, tall one!" a melodic voice called out as Anatarn slashed another warrior. "How came you here to this place, and whom do you serve?"

Anatarn spun and saw an elven woman, two steady hands on her elven blade. She had scars all down one side of her head, and she was dressed in white leather, splattered with blood, and a flowing white cloak. "Eliyan Safril, of House Safril, sent us to defend the queen and help her kin," Anatarn said as he kicked another screaming warrior down a hill and slashed another. He remembered Eliyan's fascination with his sword and decided to prove to this elf that he was here to help. "I am Anatarn Blackblade, and I serve no man, but I wield the sword Dar'kir in the name of good. My companion, Alant, is headed up the tower with Ilen'dar, the Sword of Light, to face the dark knight attacking your queen." He had never felt so out of place saying that, but the look on the woman's face said it all.

"Truly, you are all well come then, Anatarn. My name is Ari'kel Everblade, and I am Captain of the Queen's Watch. Come, let us push these barbarians back to their ships and drive them out together." The elven warrior flung her hand out and twisted four fingers, sending a gust of wind down the path that scattered the charging warriors before them.

Anatarn and Ari'kel tore through the horde, battling dark knights and warriors alike. These dark knights were no less skilled than Callen Drah—sending out tendrils of ash to burn and engulf their enemies—yet they had no prophecy around them, it seemed. Dar'kir sliced into them with ease, and though he took a good many wounds, he held his own. Anatarn couldn't help but feel sick at the scene they came upon as they rounded the corner to the docks. Bodies lay everywhere—both elven, faerie, and warrior alike—while elven ships could be seen still sinking off the shore. Five of the great black ships had smashed into the elegant white docks of the elves while black-armored warriors milled about in a throng of blades against the disheartened elves and faeries that stood fighting for their lives. Blood magic was tearing through their wards, and the fervent barbarians screamed their holy war cry as they charged. Then he saw her.

Falgrim was still charging towards the lead ship with Syn'ella right beside her. The dwarven woman stopped for nothing as she shouldered warrior after warrior out of the way, taking wound after wound, knowing that the bloodmages were the true threat to the field of battle.

"Are those your companions?" Ari'kel asked as she blasted a dark knight back with a column of ice and kicked a warrior away. A blast of fire coming in from the ships singed her arm as she spun, and she hurled a bolt of light right back, taking the bloodmage in the face.

"Yeah, and I feel really bad for those bloodmages," Anatarn said with a laugh. There were only two bloodmages left, standing together on the lead ship, working in tandem, but they were devastating the elven forces. A horrid scream echoed across the field of battle as Falgrim's axe sank into one of the bloodmages and knocked him off his feet, just as she launched herself at the other one standing with his mouth agape. The dwarven fighter was a blur of fists and knees, tumbling over and over with the black-robed figure. A cry of hope rang from the elves as both mages went down, and a shining figure rose high in the sky with a tiny sword.

"Fight on, brave elves!" Syn'ella cried out as loud as she could. "Fight for your lives, for your queen, and our victory!"

Anatarn slammed into the warriors near the ships with a hearty laugh, ignoring his many wounds. He slashed and parried, spinning with Ari'kel in a deadly circle as they laid waste to the remaining warriors. Soon, the warriors and the few dark knights that were left broke and retreated to their ships, the elves cutting as many down as they could before the ships turned and sailed off. *That was only ten dark knights*, Anatarn thought as he caught his breath. *And we dropped maybe seven of them.*

"Fall back, elves of Tsir'illia!" Ari'kel called out, her voice magnified with magic. "Let them go and let us focus on the wounded."

"Where is Alant?" Syn'ella asked as she came flying over. One side of her tiny body was covered in blood from a nasty gash, and her wings were singed. "He hasn't come down yet?"

"Alant went into the tower after that dark knight," Anatarn said. "I haven't seen him since." Before anyone else could speak, the cliffside wall of the tower exploded out in a blast of green, and two bodies could be seen falling with the rubble into the sea far below. A flaring light burned brightly as they plummeted from view.

"Alant!" Syn'ella screamed as she surged towards the cliffside. Falgrim caught her tiny body and held her fast, clutching her to her chest as tears fell down her blood-smeared face.

"Nay, brave Syn'ella, I will not lose you too."

Ari'kel ran for the tower with a contingent of elves just as another explosion of green shot up from the sea, causing the very cliffs to shake. *"No!"* Syn'ella cried out as she fought the dwarf's hold with everything she had. "I can't lose him!"

Anatarn rushed over and stood right in front of Syn'ella, holding her face still as he looked into her wide, frantic eyes. More faeries gathered as well, all whispering to each other and frowning. "You said you were soulbonded to Alant, right?" he asked, trying to get her to focus on his voice. He could see Falgrim's tears and was shaken, but he couldn't dwell on that right now.

"Ye...yes."

"Do you still feel him? Concentrate, Syn'ella; can you tell if he is alive?"

Syn'ella closed her golden eyes and took a shuddering breath. "I can! Alant is alive. Oh, Anatarn, I was so lost, but you helped me remember…thank you." Syn'ella went limp in Falgrim's arms as he let go of her face and backed up. The faeries around them all cheered, then scattered away to help the wounded.

"A faerie soulbonded to a human?" another elf asked as Falgrim took Syn'ella to a healer. This elf's dark green robes were covered in blood— most of it his—and his long white hair hung in front of his burning green eyes.

"Yes. Syn'ella told us that it is rare," Anatarn said as he looked around. The elves were gathering the dead and tending to the wounded, but Anatarn's heart sank as he saw the distant ships turning south. "The ships...they must be getting ready to hit the rest of the coastline, then assail Branthian."

"Fear not. What you did for the elves this day will not be forgotten, stranger. I am Gallus Silverspear, and I am indebted to help you in your battles from now to the end of this war or my life." The elf turned to the tower just as Ari'kel came down the path, carrying what Anatarn could only assume was the queen and a familiar silver shield. The queen raised a hand before letting it drop and going limp. The cheer that went up was even louder than before.

"Queen Tolandra lives," Ari'kel said as she came over holding the limp body of the wounded queen. Her wings were almost burnt away, and a huge slash was open on her side. "I, and any wizards that choose to help, will prepare the rest of the day to portal to the capital of Branth and fight these invaders alongside you." Ari'kel handed the silver shield to Anatarn with a sad look on her face.

"Thank you, Ari'kel," Anatarn said as he took the shield, then stumbled back. The wounds he had taken were finally catching up with him as the rush of the fight left his body. *This shield weighs almost nothing,* he thought as others helped steady him.

"Now, let us get you and the queen to those healers still capable and get you some food," Ari'kel said as Anatarn sheathed his sword. It would be a long day for most of these wounded, and he could only imagine what Alant was going through. *Zomnus be with him,* Anatarn thought as he limped over to Falgrim.

Alant charged into the queen's tower and looked around, horrified. There were bodies of both elves and faeries everywhere, some with massive holes burned through them. The sounds of steel on steel could be heard from above, as Alant searched for the stairs.

"Help her," a faint voice called from the bottom of the stairs. The elf was barely hanging on, both legs burned badly through her robe, with a deep gash in her torso. A sword was gripped in her weathered hands, and she looked to be the oldest elf Alant could ever imagine.

"Hang on, brave warrior," Alant cried, rushing towards the helpless figure.

"No warrior am I, brave knight. I am Millicent, the queen's lady-in-waiting. Go...up. Save her from that...that monster." With that, the breath escaped her broken body, and the elf was gone.

"Fiend!" Alant called out as he took the narrow stone steps two at a time. "Face me, creature of darkness!" One flight, then another, Alant raced up, his rage fueling his strength. *These elves didn't ask for this*, he thought as he rounded the next bend.

"Who comes to protect the helpless, broken queen now?" the deep voice of Samor Cah called down from above. "You only rush towards death."

I thought he was destroyed for good. The voice sounded different, less muffled to Alant. The landings were large and, at every floor, more bodies lay strewn about in death as Alant ran on. When he reached the next landing, he stopped in his tracks at the true horror that stood before him. Gone was the smoldering armor and helm of the knight he remembered. In its place was a bare skull with blazing green eyes and ancient armor that seemed battered and rent from battle.

"Run, Alant. This beast is beyond even you," Queen Tolandra called weakly from behind the Shadowknight. She raised her hands again, in absolute exhaustion, and brought up a shield as the creature swung a hammer backwards, knocking her against the stone wall with enough force to shake the tower. Tolandra cried out and slumped down, barely conscious.

"Silence, elf. This is a long-awaited rematch," Samor said as he walked towards Alant. "Honor demands it."

Alant saw that the queen was spitting blood, and her leg seemed broken as she fought to stay awake, her arm hanging limp at her side. "You will pay for all the death you have wrought, Samor Cah. I know not what you have been remade into, but I will send you back to the endless nothing." Alant drew Ilen'dar, light flaring as the blade rang with a clarion call, making the former Knight of Shad'ar step back. The Silverlord lunged forward, and their weapons clashed, sparks flying out as they fought.

"You never faced me in true battle, young one. Now you will learn why your former lord fell so easily," Samor goaded as he brought his hammer around in a deadly arc.

Alant clenched his teeth and raised the Banner of Branthian, deflecting the hammer and stepping into the large creature's reach, stabbing up into the shoulder plate. The sword flared brightly...and then nothing happened. He looked up in disbelief just as Samor's shield bashed him in the face, sending him reeling back.

"That trick worked once, but I am no longer what I once was, young fool. Now you will die." Samor Cah pressed the attack, hammering Alant's shield time and time again. While the young fighter staggered back, Samor's eyes glowed bright green as a beam shot out at Alant.

Alant raised his shield at the last second, taking the blast on the enchanted silver banner. His vision went black as he hit the stone wall behind him; he fought to stay standing as his head rang with bells. *Alright, note to self. Do not let that hit me again*, he thought as his vision cleared just in time for him to roll out of the way of that deadly hammer. Alant cursed himself as he went on the offensive, trying to get back to equal footing with the master warrior.

I let him bait me and get me angry. Stupid squire, you're better than that, he berated himself as he swung at Samor's skull and watched the creature raise his shield. *But two can play that game.*

"You're getting tired, *squire*, while I never will. Yield, and I will grant you a quick death by my weapon," Samor Cah said as he spun around and brought his hammer up from the low position.

Alant deflected the massive weapon and spun himself, coming around with his guard up again. "You know that skull looks horrible on you. At least your old helm looked impressive, but this? It just makes you look silly," Alant teased as he parried another swing and riposted quickly, then rolled again. The beginnings of a plan formed in his mind as he saw Samor's eyes glow.

"Insolent whelp!" Samor Cah raged, then blasted out again with his eyes. The beam clipped Alant's shield, tearing it from his arm, and gouged the stairs deeply, making the tower shake.

"Hey, remember, this insolent whelp killed you...twice." Alant parried with his sword now, again and again, never seeking the obvious openings that Samor was leaving. The young Silverlord knew that he couldn't wound bone; he needed something more powerful.

Samor Cah rushed Alant with a growl and pinned the young fighter against the far wall with his shield. "For that, you will die horribly, *squire*. Say goodbye." Samor's eyes charged brightly, mere inches from Alant's face.

"It's Silverlord, to you, *corpse*," Alant growled right back. He waited till the last moment and twisted free, grabbing Samor's skull and forcing it into the stone wall hard. The blast rocked them both and blew out the stone wall in a massive explosion, sending both bodies spiraling down towards the sea below. Alant fought to stay conscious as the wind whipped by his head, deafening him. He saw the body of the dark knight falling next to him, and he grabbed the armor, trying to spin the body around so it would hit the water first. He saw Samor's head shake as the beast came to and smiled as the dark knight screamed in fury, just as they slammed into the waves. There was a great emerald flash, then darkness.

Everything hurt. That was the first thing Alant knew as he came to. He tried to stand but couldn't move his arms. "What..." he started to say as a boot landed into his gut.

"Oh, look, they're awake," a deep voice said mockingly.

Alant tried to focus and saw a huge figure standing over him, a sword leveled at his throat, poised to strike. He tried to move again and realized that his arms were tied behind his back. He was sitting on a wooden floor, and the whole room was rocking gently back and forth. *A ship*, he rationalized as his vision cleared.

"Have you no honor, Gravil Kar?" the voice of Samor Cah said from across the room. You would attack a helpless enemy?"

"You speak of honor? You, who are now a walking horror to everyone's eyes?" the voice of Gravil accused.

Alant looked and saw that Gravil Kar was indeed another Shadowknight, the smoldering armor and helm recognizable anywhere. This Knight of Shad'ar had long blond hair spilling from his helm at the back. Alant strained against his bonds with everything he had, yet the ropes were too strong. Even with his size and strength, he couldn't break free.

"Yes, I speak of honor. It is all we have left after pledging our very souls to that madman," Samor said, looking over at Alant. "Besides, he is mine to kill."

"Well, you both will have to wait until we meet up with the rest of the fleet attacking Branthian. Reasen Dhal will know what to do with you."

CHAPTER NINE — IT'S ALWAYS DARKEST...

Fields Outside of Branth, Nation of Branthian.

She watched the fire explode in the distant night sky and scowled. They had docked hours ago and prepared for the dark ships, but the head sorcerer, Gerick Eldon, refused to believe how dangerous the bloodmages could be, despite even Ereval saying so. Hylana dodged a spear and grabbed her amethyst. "Litar!" she yelled, calling upon the words of power and sending a blast of lightning through the ranks of barbaric warriors. Two young sorcerers ran toward her, pursued by a Shadowknight, and cried out for help. Before she could respond, roots exploded up from the ground, tangling the dark knight and stopping his charge cold.

"Go back to the ground, foul beast!" Ereval shouted as his magic dragged the dark knight into the dirt and closed over him. Before she could offer thanks, an arrow took the elven archmage in the leg, and he spun, lashing out with a spear of light, blasting four archers away. "Are you both alright?" Ereval asked the young sorcerers as he limped over.

"Yes. Thank you, Archmage," Yalen said, bent over and out of breath. He was the youngest sorcerer in the castle, and fear was etched across his youthful face.

"Gerick has fallen, my lady," the other blurted out, fear dancing across her blue eyes as well. Lowen was a dedicated sorceress, studying the element of wind primarily. "You are the new High Sorcerer...er...Sorceress."

Hylana closed her eyes for a brief moment, then focused on the younglings. "Damn fool didn't listen. Alright, both of you get back to the gates, assist with the healing, and tell King Danrae that I said we need to fall back." Hylana turned to Ereval as he healed his leg, then patted the young ones on the head. "How about you, Ereval. Are you good?" Hylana knew that casting magic was exhausting, and she was pushing herself as it was. Ereval had been casting much more and still showed no signs of slowing down.

"I'm fine, or as close to fine as I'm going to get in battle. Elven wizards can cast a bit more than you sorcerers, but not much more. An archmage, a bit more than that."

"Here they come, High Sorceress," one of her sorcerers, Balo Ferin, called back to her as the tide of barbaric warriors surged forth past the dark knights and howled their vengeance. There had to be more than a dozen Shadowknights, but these barbarians were almost worse with their numbers. Balo grasped his own stone—a small garnet— and shouted a word of power, spinning in his red robes and sending flames in a cone towards the oncoming horde. Those flames met a wind wall and were brushed back into the sorcerer's face; he fell screaming as Ereval rushed to help him.

"Damn those bloodmages to the hells," Hylana cursed as she threw her wall of earth at the oncoming warriors. Normally, the sorcerers would cancel each other out, but Branthian couldn't ward off their bloodmagic, keeping most of the sorcerers in the back and out of the fight. "We need to fall back!" Even as she called out the command, she knew they weren't going to be able to—not with this many warriors charging them. Just as she was going to suggest a fruitless plan, a blaring horn call split the night.

The ground thundered with hooves, and the air cried with more horns as the rest of the Knights of the Realm came charging out across the plains from the safety of Branth, King Danrae at their head. "Damn that man, too!" Hylana said with a smile.

"He does know how to make an entrance, doesn't he?" Ereval said as he lifted a stone and hurled it at the charging warriors.

"Yes, but our advantage was saving those knights for the ambush as we fell back," the high sorceress said. "Now, there is no help if the fallback runs into problems." Hylana shrugged and strode out to the front, determined to save as many Branthian warriors as possible before these barbaric hordes overwhelmed them. She rolled out of the way of a massive shard of ice and grasped her amethyst tightly, slamming the ground with her other hand for balance. "Direnar!" she cried out, lifting a huge chunk of the very ground and slamming it back down, causing the charge to falter and almost break as the black warriors stumbled and lost their feet.

"Down!" Ereval shouted as he sent out a blade of light to pierce the Shadowknight that was almost on her. The light hit the smoldering armor and flared in the night, the dark knight screaming in agony and dropping to his knees as the Branthian guard hacked at him, finally dropping the creature.

"To the High Sorceress!" Lowen called out as she ran over and helped Hylana up. More sorcerers rallied to her; together, they stood their ground as the Knights of the Realm ran interference for the others to retreat to the main gates.

"Archmage!" Yalen called out in warning as a stream of ash from a Shadowknight's blade came winding through the night towards Ereval, but the elf had no time, caught flatfooted, and engaged with two other warriors. Yalen leapt in the path of the ash, his yellow stone flaring as he cried out his word of power. "Ilren!" Light flared, stopping the ash momentarily, but the stream plowed into the tiny shield of light, blasting through and engulfing the young boy mid-air.

"No!" Ereval screamed, flicking his fingers and bringing his other fist down, striking the Knight of Shad'ar with a bolt of lightning that split the night sky. He scooped up the young boy and fell back. He tried to heal the boy, but his limits were almost reached; he couldn't stop the dark ash from its burning course. Tears of silver fell upon the dying child as the elven archmage knelt in the burnt grass. "Hear me, Amara. No other child will die this day while I draw breath," he vowed as he stood and dug down deep.

Hylana caught his gaze and nodded, sharing his resolve. "Let us go; someone has to guard the knights' retreat. It might as well be us, right?" she asked.

"Not this day," a melodic voice called behind them as Ari'kel stepped through a portal with Syn'ella. More portals were opening across the field as elven wizards stepped through, most already casting as they walked upon the ruined grass. The horde was slowed, and the branthians fell back as quickly as possible, with the knights behind them covered by the newly arrived wizards.

"Syn'ella!" Hylana called out in wonder as she fell back as well now. "You are well come indeed, but I fear that even this may not be enough to get us safely back to the castle with these bloodmages." Hylana counted at least ten elven wizards, a force to be reckoned with for sure, but the bloodmages would be ready for magic of any kind.

“We have a secret weapon against them,” Anatarn said, as he stepped through a portal with Gallus Silverspear. As if on cue, a female dwarf charged straight out of a portal into the oncoming horde and made a hole, aiming straight for the bloodmage behind them.

“Where is Alant?” Hylana asked, fearful at his absence and noting the shield Anatarn now wore on his arm.

Syn’ella flew up to her, the tiny faerie’s eyes swollen with tears. “He fell with the Knight of Shad’ar that was attacking the queen. He yet lives, I can feel him, but I know not where except north.”

“And the queen?” Ereval asked, his eyes scanning the night for the dark knights.

“She lives, if barely,” Syn’ella said as she drew her slim sword and guarded Hylana.

“Forces to the left,” Gallus called out as he pointed and sent a display of light into the sky. It illuminated their flank and showed the forces of the dark knights that had fallen back. They had taken the time to circle around and had the retreat almost blocked.

“That’s why we’ve been doing so well, their heavy hitters pulled back to encircle us,” Ereval said with a frown.

“We’ve been doing well?” Hylana asked sarcastically as she saw the king ride up. “Your Majesty, I told you to stay in the castle.”

“My subjects needed help, and I am still an able fighter, High Sorceress,” King Danrae said with a smile. “Now, rally the Knights of the Realm and let us get these tired warriors into the castle before the dark knights cut us off for good.” The king kicked his horse forward and was followed by the contingent of knights.

“Wait for me, King Danrae,” Ereval yelled as he grabbed a riderless horse—its rider slain in battle—and followed.

Hylana rallied the remaining sorcerers and elven wizards to keep the warriors safe from the barbaric warriors still advancing, and breathed a sigh of relief when she noticed there seemed to be only a couple of the bloodmages left. She watched as Anatarn and Syn'ella went to help battle the Knights of Shad'ar and felt herself relax a tiny bit. *We might make it to the castle*, she thought as she saw Falgrim come out of the fighting with Lowen helping her. Then she heard what she had dreaded all this time.

"The King is down!" Ereval's voice echoed across the battlefield as bright light flared, pushing the dark knights back for a moment.

With the flare of light, Hylana could see that the dark knights were cutting the Knights of the Realm down quickly. These undead knights had hundreds of years of experience, and their sword work was masterful. By themselves, the Branthian forces had been holding their own, but with the undead knights all together like that, they were almost unstoppable. It helped that they didn't feel pain or get tired, either. "Lirial!" she called out, using the word of power that would create a massive globe of light. She gripped her amethyst as her vision blurred, the exertion of magic finally taking its toll on her.

"Easy there, lass," Falgrim said as she caught her. "Let's get you inside before you take a dirt nap, alright?" They fell back towards the castle, meeting the retreating Knights of the Realm before seeing the gate. "Anatarn, what happened?" Falgrim asked as she helped Hylana.

"The king took a vicious hit from one of those smoke swords. The wound is black and seems like it is eating him," Anatarn said, as he helped a knight off his wounded horse. "I've got to get back in there. Dar'kir is one of the only things hurting those knights."

“Be safe, Love,” Falgrim said, then looked at Hylana with narrowed eyes. “You heard nothing.”

Hylana laughed weakly and nodded as Ereval and Syn’ella came over with two knights carrying the king. His breastplate was gone, and a horrible black wound festered across his abdomen. The wound pulsed with evil, and she could almost feel the darkness radiating from it.

“I’ve seen a wound like this on Alant before. He lasted almost two days before they could heal him,” Syn’ella said with a deep sadness in her melodic voice. She looked ragged, with flecks of blood covering her vibrant wings.

“I can’t save him, I’m near exhaustion as it is,” Ereval admitted, “but I can show Ari’kel and some others how to do it.”

“It won’t matter if we can’t get in the castle,” Lowen said, fear rising in her voice. “Look!”

Hylana gave Falgrim a nod of thanks, looked back where Lowen was pointing, and saw the Knights of Shad’ar closing the flank in the now dwindling light from her spell. Anatarn was battling fiercely with the Knights of the Realm, but the dark knights were too many and too skilled. Just as the fading light sputtered out, cloaking the battlefield in darkness once more, a distant horn sounded from behind the dark knights.

“I’d know that horn anywhere!” Falgrim shouted. “The dwarves are here!”

Hylana’s breath caught when another horn blasted in the night air; confusion hit the dark knights as battle commenced behind them. Caught between enemies, the dark knights faltered, leaving an opening for the forces of Branthian to get to the safety of the castle. “Fall back, brave warriors! To the castle!” she cried out, using her magic to shield those whom she could. Hylana could feel exhaustion starting to cripple her; she didn’t have much energy left. The dwarves and knights took heavy losses covering their retreat, but—in the end—the Knights of Shad'ar were broken and the gates slammed shut, braced from within.

"Falgrim! You're alive," Belsa called out as the dwarven regiment took count of their fallen in the outer courtyard. The stout dwarven warrior came over to Hylana and Falgrim; she was covered in blood, most of it hers.

"And you're just in time, girl. Thank the Forge," Falgrim said honestly.

"Thank the knights from Oliar. They kept up with our pace to get here as fast as we could." Belsa looked at Hylana with a curious glance. "Sorceress, I take it?"

"High Sorceress now, unfortunately," Hylana said, with a pang of sadness for her fallen friends and students. She saw the knights and dwarves working together, and it brought a smile to her lips. "Thank you for coming to our aid, good dwarf. Branthian owes you."

"Thank Alant. He helped us just as much against the dead. Speaking of the dead," Belsa said. "You two need to see something." The dwarf motioned them to climb the tower near the gate. Once they were at the top, Belsa pointed out to the horizon.

Even through the darkness, Hylana could make out a black mass, deeper than night, moving towards them. "What is that?"

"It's a black storm coming out of the Endless Wastes with an army of the dead behind it, and it looks like it is coming right here." Belsa shivered and looked away.

"They're attacking the gates!" a cry came from below as the warriors moved the wounded into the inner courtyard.

Hylana could see Ereval and Ari'kel healing the king and knew they couldn't stop now. The High Sorceress took two steps and almost fainted, caught by Falgrim.

“Yer gonna take a dirt nap if you keep using that magic, girlie.” Falgrim helped her down the stairs and into the yard, just as Ereval sat down with limp arms. The elven archmage had been casting nonstop for a long time and finally reached his limit.

Hylana’s eyes went wide when ash started seeping through the crack in the massive gates, and the smell of burning wood filled the air. “We have to get the king inside, now!”

“We... can’t move... him yet. If Ari’kel stops, it will...rebound and consume him instantly,” Ereval said, standing up with help from Lowen.

Hylana looked around at the exhausted sorcerers and frowned. There wasn’t anyone not wiped out who could hold those gates with magic. If those gates fell, they would storm the outer courtyard and slay the wounded king.

“Dwarves! Form up!” Belsa cried out as she stomped past Hylana. “Let’s hold that gate to the last dwarf!”

“We’re with you, good lady,” Knight-Commander Coran said, limping with two other Knights of the Realm.

“Wait,” Ereval said, holding up his hand. “If you dwarves... can open those gates quickly, I can buy... us some time,” the archmage said through gritted teeth. “No more shall fall before the dawn...while I draw breath.”

“Aye, we can do that,” Falgrim said as Anatarn waved at her from across the yard.

“Oh, and tell him...about the bond, dear dwarf. It’s as plain...to me as the sunrise.”

Hylana had a pit in her stomach, but she was so exhausted, there was nothing she could do but watch. “Ereval...what?”

“Hylana Brendal of Branthian, it was the... greatest honor to observe you casting magic as well as any elf...and for valiant reasons. Your name will forever be... in the elven books of heroines." Ereval stood on his own two feet and went to the gate, taking a deep breath and steadying himself. "Tell my sister that... I will see her in the Forever Lands."

The dwarves threw open the gates as the dark knights and barbaric warriors stumbled in, and Ereval dropped to his knees, fists into the ground. *"No more!"* Ereval cried out as his body glowed briefly, then exploded outward, blasting the dark forces with bright light and throwing them back over twenty feet while they burned. Their ruined bodies tumbling as the dwarves pushed the gates back and braced them once more.

"Ereval!"

"They are withdrawing!" someone called from the battlements, but Hylana couldn't take her eyes from where Ereval once stood. The elven archmage was simply…gone.

"Life magic," Gallus sobbed next to her as he came over. "I've never seen it so powerful before. He gave his very being to the magic that blasted our foes."

Hylana fell to her knees, and tears fell as King Danrae drew a deep healing breath. She hadn't been strong enough to save the king—to do what Ereval had done—and that weighed heavily on her soul in the moment. *I swear to you, Amara, that I will not be found wanting again. Ereval has shown me what true courage is, and I will not fail a second time,* she thought as the dwarves braced the gates and set watch with the knights of Oliar.

Capital City of Llor, Nation of Lorant

She opened her eyes and tried to sit up. That was her first mistake. Eliyan groaned loudly and wrapped her arms around her stomach as everything decided to hurt all at once. It felt like her very soul was cracked.

"Take it easy there, little one," Alsan said from the door as she came in. "You are going to need your rest for at least another day or two."

"Why aren't I dead?" Eliyan asked, genuinely confused. "I remember seeing your face, then a bright light. I assumed it was the Forever Lands welcoming me home."

"The Forever Lands?" Alsan asked, sitting down next to the elven healer, and feeling her head.

"Yes. When elves die, they pass into a place where all their past mistakes are forgiven. It's where Amara dwells."

"The Goddess of Nature and Magic?"

"Yes. The elves are her children." Eliyan fought again to sit up, and this time only bit her lip at the pain. "I'll ask again. How am I alive?"

"Alsan saved you by giving you some of her life," Ongril said as he came into the room. "And if you *ever* try that again, I will kill you myself." The elven steward looked at Alsan with a disapproving glance and scowled at Eliyan.

"Alsan? But...wait. You are a sorcerer?" It was the only thing that made sense. Yet, she didn't have a stone, and Eliyan heard no words of power.

"No. I...." Alsan looked to Ongril and hung her head. "It's part of my dirty little secret. My mother was supposedly some powerful half-elven wizard," she said, a weary smile on her face. "I've never learned much—father refused to talk about it outright—but I learned some things by reading the old elven books in father's private library. It was a scandal and was buried so deeply that no one was allowed to speak of it. I do know that he paid her off and she left...but that's all I know

"But how did you know to do that?" Eliyan asked, a wrinkle on her pale brow now.

"I...I didn't. I just knew that I had to save you, and when I placed my hands on you, they started glowing. I just poured myself into you."

"That's why you look so tired," Eliyan said. "Your first casting is always the hardest, but to do it that way...." At that moment, the elven healer's eyes went wide as she remembered the dire situation that made her try to hold a portal for so long. "The queen! Did they save her?"

"I have heard from Tolandra, yes," Ongril said as he sat on the other side of Eliyan. "Although Alant fell into the sea with that foul creature. Syn'ella said she can still feel him; he is alive, at least."

"You don't look like that is all the news you have to share, though, Ongril." Eliyan could see the worry etched on his face still.

"Branthian was attacked as well, and the capital is under siege. Ereval is exhausted, but the sorcerers aren't much better. They had bloodmages and a score of dark knights as well as hundreds of barbaric, holy warriors."

"So, when do we leave?" Eliyan said, trying to swing her legs over the side of the bed. Once again, her body voiced its extreme displeasure, and she almost lost consciousness.

"You're not going anywhere, let alone using magic to get there," Ongril said, laying her back down. "We'll see in another day or so." He patted her head and got up, blew a kiss to Alsan, and closed the door behind him.

"You know, Alsan," Eliyan said, with a smirk once the door was closed. "I may not be able to cast a portal, but I bet you would be able to learn that spell fast." The women shared a devious smile.

"I bet we would've been great friends growing up, Eliyan," Alsan said. "I know you want to go help your friends, but let's wait at least a couple of hours, alright?"

"I guess...but we can't tell Ongril."

"Agreed."

Black Ship, Somewhere Off the Coast of Alian'tir.

He watched the young squire struggle against his bonds again for the hundredth time to no avail. Samor Cah shook his skull and sighed, even though he didn't need to breathe. "I can't believe you haven't broken free yet, squire," Samor said in a mocking tone. They were both bound with heavy rope, even though it would never hold the Knight of Shad'ar.

"You could be free anytime you wish," Alant said in the dark corner. "You could break free and kill me right here and now."

"You don't understand honor then, whelp," Samor Cah spat out. "You beat me the first time from behind, then the second time you tricked me. *When* I kill you, you will be healthy and ready, with that sword in your hand."

"Well, that won't happen if your friends kill me first," Alant said as he wriggled around in his bonds. "Unless they have the same twisted sense of honor that you have."

Samor held his words on that account, mainly because he wasn't at all sure he could answer confidently. He had noticed that some of his former Knights of Shad'ar had fallen from their honorable upbringing, and he wasn't sure why. *Honor was ingrained into us back when we were Dragonknights of Jal'rien, and that didn't just go away,* he thought. *Or did it?*

"Well, well, what do we have here?" a shadowy voice called from the stairs.

Samor peered into the darkness as a small light flared, showing a sorcerer of Raer'drin—probably a bloodmage—holding that accursed sword that had slain him; Ilen'dar, the Sword of Light. The man had long blond hair and piercing green eyes, wearing a large bloodstone around his neck. He wasn't aware of any sorcerers left on the ship when they were taken aboard and bound down here, though he wasn't particularly coherent when that happened.

"You will find out, sorcerer, if I ever get free," Alant said with a bravado that seemed out of place.

The man grabbed the blood red stone and ran his finger along the blade as he walked, using the blood to fuel his magic further, lighting up the room like the dawn. "It seems like we have a captive knight *and* an abomination," the man said, ignoring Alant's outburst. He leveled the Sword of Light at Samor's chest and poked the dark knight.

"Name thyself, weakling," Samor said. "Fight me like a man of honor, and I will give you a swift death."

"I am Reasen Dhal, Highmage to Archmage Raer'dreth himself, and you are to be brought before him, dead or alive."

The bloodmage flicked the sword against Samor's skull and laughed, pulling back for a finishing blow.

The sword hurt just by touching him, but, just like at the tower, he tried to show nothing outwardly. The sword wouldn't slay him outright in this new form, but it still hurt like the hells. It would still vaporize most undead—like his former knights—but he was protected at least. "You would slay me, bound and helpless?" Samor asked with a hint of humor in his hollow voice.

Reason stopped and smirked. "Of course. I'm not stupid, fallen knight."

"Good. Then, like those elves at the tower that attacked me from behind, you don't deserve an honorable death." Samor's eyes flared green as they shot out into Reason's face. The bloodmage fell back, screaming, and landed against the far wall, sliding down lifeless in a heartbeat as the fire burned away his head. Samor flexed once and snapped the ropes binding him, standing quickly and striding towards Alant. "They will be coming, take your sword and prepare, whelp. We're going to have to fight our way out."

"Why are you helping me?" Alant asked as he gathered his fallen sword and flexed his arms.

"Because I want to kill you. If I don't help you get out of here, one of my former knights might do it, and that I will not allow." Samor Cah had no more time for the whelp as he heard the heavy steps of the knights coming down thc stairs. He didn't have his hammer, but he had been fighting for over two hundred years; he could fight with almost anything. The former Dark Knight went forward to meet his brethren and waited to see what they would do.

"Stand down, abomination, or be destroyed," one of the dark knights said as he leveled his sword of shadows at Samor.

"I do not want to make you enemies, brothers, but this whelp is mine to kill. Let us go, and I will not stand in the way of your conquest." Samor didn't think it would work—he could already see one of the knights trying to flank them. "Fine. Battle it is. Will none of you give me a weapon to fight with then? For honor?"

"We do not hold to honor these days. You are the enemy, Samor. You have been declared a liability and are to be destroyed." The knight strode forward and raised his sword as the other three spread out.

Samor Cah punched him straight in the chest so fast that the knight couldn't even get his shield up in time. Samor's preternatural strength sent the dark knight flying onto his back, a massive dent in the shadowy armor. Samor stepped sideways as another knight swung and grabbed her wrist, twisting her arm and taking her sword. Samor back-handed her hard, sending her flying. The Knights of Shad'ar were strong, but Samor was something else entirely now. Not much could stand against him.

"You would attack your own kind, Samor?" one of the knights asked as he sent a line of ash from his sword towards Samor.

Alant stepped in the way and raised Ilen'dar, taking the ash on the blade. The sword flared brightly, and he lunged, taking the knight in the helm. The blade went through, and the knight screamed horribly, then the armor clattered to the deck, empty.

"Did I scream like that when you killed me?" Samor asked the young whelp as he kicked out at the last knight, catching him in the sternum and folding the knight over.

"Do you want the truth?" Alant asked with a smile.

"Never mind," Samor said begrudgingly. He had to admit, the young squire was good with a sword, and as he saw him fight, he could see a lot of his former self in the boy. They fought up the stairs, dispatching the knights as they went.

Samor watched as Alant finished the knights where they stood, waiting for them to be ready before he swung with his blade. The flare of light sent them to the ether instead of their soulgems, and Samor felt a pang of jealousy; they were finally free. Soon, the unlikely pair was on the main deck, the sea breeze washing over his skull. Of all the things he couldn't feel anymore, he missed the wind the most.

"You know, it is a shame I have to kill you. You remind me a lot of myself when I was young," Samor said quietly.

Before Alant could reply, the air shimmered and a portal opened, with three bloodmages stepping through. One quickly grabbed his bloodstone and cast a binding spell, wrapping Alant's arms tight and lifting him in the air.

"Raer'dreth wants both of you right now, abomination," the second one said as he clutched his stone ready to cast, but Samor was faster.

Samor lashed out with his fist and punched through the man's chest in a spray of blood. "The boy is mine to kill!" Samor yelled as both remaining bloodmages backed up in horror.

The bloodmages each grabbed their bloodstones and quickly bent down to smear their comrade's blood on their hands as they cast, screaming the words of power in unison. "Stadar!" The enhanced magic reached out and grabbed the dark knight, binding his arms, legs, and even his eyes in iron and holding him fast. Struggle as he might, the bloodmagic held him captive. He felt them drag him, and then the sensation of magic washed over him.

The portal, he thought as he struggled uselessly. He relaxed, saving his strength for the audience with his former master. He only hoped that it went better than the last time.

Ruins of Fort Kaldrin, Nation of Branthian

She watched the dark shadow storm wash over the trees and plants on its continued path toward the capital of Branthian. The knights of the fallen fort were riding in the distance toward their king as the dead shuffled all around her, stumbling over the bones of those not quick enough to flee. Her master's lingering spell worked its magic still, as the bodies of the fallen knights stood, still grasping their swords and shields. They fell in behind her as she trudged on, her mind wandering now as it recalled that fateful day.

Callen Drah rode behind the first shadow storm with her brothers and sisters in arms—dragonknights all—after they had sworn fealty to Raer'dreth. Jal'rien had been wiped out quickly, the lush trees and pools of crystal-clear water erased as if they had never been there; the vegetation turning to a lifeless grey. Buildings crumbled here and there as the storm of dark shadows tore around them. Callen and her fellow knights knew not what they had signed up for, yet they would soon enough.

Their first death was the fastest; the soul didn't need help in this first transition, the soulgem being created out of the slain body, crystallizing into gems situated around the dark archmage as he sat directing his spell. When one of her brothers was cut down by a distant wizard, the body formed in front of them out of a fallen corpse, the new armor and sword manifesting out of the very shadows that slew the warrior.

Horrified as they were, the former dragonknights knew that this was the price of their treason; the price of an unholy pact. They slew the remaining enemies that didn't succumb to the shadow storm and always rose again to keep going, thanks to Raer'dreth's magic. When the other archmages found out the extent of his destruction, they banished him, sending him over the wide sea to a barren continent; or so they thought.

A scream brought Callen out of her reflection in time to see a small band of knights standing against the horde of the dead. They had eluded the swirling storm and stood now against the shuffling horror. She saw the head knight give a small patch to another knight on a horse and whisper something, then turn toward the dead and swing his massive sword and lock eyes with her. The knight on the horse rode hard behind the refugees.

"Face me, creature of the dark, and die with honor on the blade of a Knight of the Realm. I am Knight-Captain Feskar, and I challenge you," the knight called out as he battled the dead surging around him.

Callen Drah tried to rush forward, but the swarm of the dead was too thick. "Leave this knight to *me*," she called out to the swarming dead, yet they no longer listened to her voice. She watched helplessly as the dead dragged him down, their weapons cleaving the armor from him little by little before she could get to him. Finally getting there as he was stabbed over and over, Callen looked down as he breathed his last.

"Cow...ard," the knight whispered before the dead silenced him forever.

Callen kicked out at the swarm of dead, clearing Feskar's body, and screaming her frustration. The only thing she had left was her honor, and now she couldn't even keep that. The fallen knight's word stung deeper than she would have thought; she hacked at the dead to let out her rage. It wasn't until she saw the body of the knight slowly sit up that true revulsion overtook her.

"No," Callen Drah said simply. "Not this one." She swung her blade across the risen body, cutting it in two as it fell apart at her feet. The dead ignored her and continued toward Branthian as she stared down at the broken corpse. *Is this what I've become?* she thought. Callen sheathed her weapon and walked on, determined to find the peace she had granted to the fallen knight and break free of Raer'dreth's control.

CHAPTER TEN — ...BEFORE THE DAWN

Inner Courtyard, Castle Branth

She stepped through the portal holding the grieving elven wizard on her arm and hoped that Castle Branth hadn't fallen. Tolandra Asil was still in rough shape but had gained enough rest to be useful once more. When Kysen Drial, the Lady of Dyln'ir, had come to heal her after the attack, the queen thought the worst was over. She should have known better. The sound of weapons being drawn snapped her out of her thoughts and back to the present.

"It is Queen Tolandra and Lady Kysen, hold your weapons, friends," Tolandra said weakly as the portal snapped shut behind her. The inner courtyard was a mess, with tents and a makeshift hospital set up on the muddy ground.

"My Queen!" Syn'ella called out, flying over and helping her. "You look terrible."

Tolandra smiled at the sound of Syn'ella's voice. The queen looked ragged and, though her clothes seemed fresh and clean, her body seemed broken beneath them. Bandages and splints still held her bones tight as the healing spells worked to keep her together. They had to be used over time; too many spells cast too fast, and she would become useless, her body flying into shock. Compared to Kysen, however, the queen seemed to shine.

"Where?" the lady of the shining city asked in a broken voice. Lady Kysen's long white hair was tied in a ponytail, and her amethyst eyes were swollen and tear-filled. Her beautiful dress was stained with mud, and her body was wracked by sobs as she fell to her knees.

"We have wounded!" Grym called out, the flamboyant dwarven writer rushing to Kysen's aid.

Tolandra's heart almost broke right there. She had heard stories of when soulbonds lose their partner to death, but had never witnessed one herself. Soulbonds were rare, and most usually died together from old age. "She's not..." but before Tolandra could finish, Syn'ella was there, taking Kysen's hand and leading her away. "I've got her, My Queen. Over here, brave Kysen. I have you."

"She's not wounded?" Grym asked as the other dwarves put away their weapons and sent for the High Sorceress.

"No. She was soulbonded to Ereval. She felt him die." Tolandra could only imagine the pain and loss Kysen was going through—what Syn'ella would go through when Alant died from old age, and the faerie kept living. Faeries could live to be very old, and humans were but a passing blink to most of them.

"Ah…we call it Heartbonded. It is rare among dwarves, but I get it now. I've seen grief like that once before...it can be crushing. Me name is Haragrym Wordsplitter...but you can call me Grym, fair queen."

Tolandra looked down at the dwarf and smiled at the foppish warrior. His wide, gold-brimmed hat was crumpled, and he had a long mustache curled up at the ends. "How goes the war here, Grym?" the queen asked as Hylana walked down the stone stairs towards them.

"Not well. The city is under siege, and there is a dark storm a-coming," Grym said as he bowed low and then took his leave.

"You are well come, Queen Tolandra, but shouldn't you be resting?" Hylana asked as she came over and led the queen up to the battlements.

"I couldn't stay safe in Tsir'illia when our people fight to survive. Where my people go, I go to help as well," Tolandra said, rubbing her swollen arm and adjusting the splint. She crooked her fingers slightly and sent tendrils of healing into her arm again, a little bit at a time. "What is this about a storm?"

Hylana pointed at the glowing horizon, the sun finally coming up and revealing the dark storm shadowing it. With a little light behind it, the shadow storm seemed inevitable and all-consuming.

"Amara, save us," the queen prayed as she saw what was coming. Tolandra had never seen anything like it, but had heard the stories of the Endless Wastes like any wizard training in Tsir'illia. "It is almost here."

"Yes. Fort Kaldrin and what was left of the villages have been evacuated and have fallen back here, but we need a distraction to get them inside the castle," Hylana said, her voice weary and quiet. "I'm sorry about Ereval. I wasn't strong enough to save us, so he..."

Tolandra wrapped the High Sorceress in a tight embrace, feeling the woman's pain from here. "You are stronger than you know. Ereval did what he did to save the people that he had come to admire. There is no better reason to sacrifice oneself." Tolandra wiped away a tear from Hylana's face. "Now. Let's get all the available wizards and sorcerers up here as fast as we can. After a short rest, we will try to stop that thing."

"What about the refugees?" Hylana asked as she broke away from the queen and fixed her robes.

"Leave that to us," a gruff female voice said, as more figures came up the stone stairs. It was the female dwarf and the black-dressed warrior who had saved her people at the tower. "I'm Falgrim, and this is Anatarn," Falgrim said.

"It is nice to meet the warriors that saved my people," Tolandra said with a bow. She could see the magic between them and knew that they were also soulbonded—or heartbonded, as the dwarf had called it. The man in black also had an elven blade that gleamed in her vision and, if she wasn't mistaken, it was the twin to Ilen'dar. "Is that Dar'kir?" Tolandra asked as she walked closer.

"Yes, Eliyan said it was elven. Do you know this sword, Your Highness?" Anatarn asked.

"Eliyan? Is my niece here then?"

"No, she is still in Lorant with Ongril and his lady friend, Your Highness," Falgrim said. "She opened a portal to send us all to your tower."

Tolandra's head was spinning. "All? You must be mistaken." There were so many things wrong with that entire sentence that she couldn't possibly have had enough time to start. "No matter. Good dwarf. If we all live through this, you and I are getting a good, stiff drink together," Tolandra said. "For now, though, get those people inside the castle and give us time to stop that storm."

"You got it, Your Highness," Falgrim said without tact, as she pulled Anatarn after her.

Syn'ella held Kysen's shoulders as the wizard sobbed into the dirt, the elf's hands digging down, trying to save some of the ashes left behind of her beloved Ereval. "We have to go, Lady Kysen. It's not safe in the courtyard." Syn'ella looked around and saw the dwarves and knights coming in formation. "Alright, we have to go now...it looks like things are getting bad."

"We're opening up that gate, Syn'ella. Get the lady up to the battlements and guard them while they do their magic thingy in case they break through," Falgrim said, waggling her fingers to imitate the wizards and sorcerers.

"I can...help them," Kysen said weakly, clutching a clump of dirt to her chest as she rose. She walked past the warriors and knights with her head down, her tears falling with every step.

"No one will get past me, Falgrim," Syn'ella said, drawing her blade and flying backwards. "Just come back in one piece, alright?" Syn'ella watched them go and tried not to give in to the despair growing in her tiny chest. She missed Alant so much and just wished she could go to him. The tiny faerie warrior flew beside Kysen and helped the wizard to the battlements.

"Keep him with you always, Syn'ella," Kysen whispered. "Never let him out of your sight."

Syn'ella felt heartbroken at Kysen's loss. She knew how it felt to just lose Alant for the moment. She couldn't even fathom what she would feel like if her bond were to die. Silver tears fell as she flew into Kysen's shoulders and hugged the elven wizard tight. "I'm so, so sorry, Kysen. I saw him cast that spell… he gave himself to save us all." Syn'ella felt a glow spread between them and closed her eyes, letting go. It spread from her to Kysen and felt like she shared a little piece of herself.

Kysen stopped and opened her eyes a little more, almost like she was waking up from a fog. "It... It's alright, Syn'ella. I'm...I'm going to be alright, I think. Thank you for sharing that with me. I think you just helped me through the worst parts, though I'm not sure how."

"I think I shared my soulbond with you...or at least a fraction of it."

"Yes...I can feel it here," Kysen said, pointing to her chest. "It's mending the rupture to my own inside. Well, that is new. Don't tell anyone else until we can discuss this, alright?"

Syn'ella nodded, a little lost as to what had happened herself. When they got to the top, she could see the sorcerers and wizards working together to prepare for the mass spell. The faerie warrior could see the storm coming even closer, almost to the edges of the city below. She turned and looked over the battlements to see the Branthian forces push the dark warriors back and give the refugees time to get to safety. With the light of the coming dawn, she swore she could see Falgrim and Anatarn in the front as spells flew and bloodmages died, the Banner of Branthian acting as a beacon to the Knights of the Realm.

Chanting brought her back to the task at hand, and Syn'ella saw the men and women start the spell, the elves twirling their fingers as the sorcerers uttered their words of power. Stones glowed and magic swirled, all gathering around Queen Tolandra Asil. The queen threw out her arms, and a massive light channeled through her, gathering in intensity and size.

"No... not again," Kysen said as she walked towards Tolandra. Lady Drial kept channeling her portion of the spell, but grabbed Tolandra's arm and turned to smile sadly at Syn'ella. *Thank you*, she mouthed to the faerie warrior as she closed her eyes and glowed even brighter.

"Kysen...what...no!" Tolandra cried out as the glow faded from her and intensified around the Lady of Dyln'ir.

Syn'ella flew over, but the queen held up a hand to forestall her.

"Wait, Syn'ella. If anything disrupts her now, the spell will fail."

The faerie warrior watched in horror as some of the sorcerers weakened and fell, their dead stares looking up at nothing as their life fueled the ritual. Some simply fell moaning, while others turned to ash, yet the magic kept pouring through Kysen and slammed into the dark storm with a fury unrivaled in this lifetime.

"For him, I Banish Thee!" Kysen screamed into the dark storm. The explosion when the two magical forces met shook the castle as Kysen dissolved into light itself, her last smile one of peace.

Tolandra collapsed as the magic faded, wheezing and shaking. Ky..sen"

"Queen Tolandra!" a melodic voice called out as figures ran up the stone steps.

"Eliyan!" Syn'ella called out as she saw the elven healer and the queen of Lorant come up behind Falgrim and Anatarn. Another knight was behind them as well, holding back and carrying his helm in the crook of his arm. Syn'ella saw Eliyan rush to Tolandra and pour healing energy into the half-faerie queen, bringing her breathing back to normal.

"Syn'ella," Falgrim said somberly.

The faerie warrior's stomach dropped at the tone, and she quickly focused on Alant, fearing the worst. With a sigh of relief, she felt him still strong and vibrant, yet couldn't locate him...something was blocking her. "What is it, Falgrim?" she asked as she flew over. The remaining sorcerers and wizards were helping those who had survived the powerful casting and resting themselves.

"This knight has something for you." Falgrim sniffed and backed away.

Syn'ella had never heard Falgrim sound sad before, and she approached the knight with trepidation. "What is it, brave Knight of the Realm?"

"I am Knight-Commander Terran Lawson, Brave Syn'ella. I was there when you fought, Knight-Captain Feskar," the exhausted knight said, his grey eyes downcast as he shuffled his armored feet. Slowly, the knight took something from his satchel and cradled it lovingly before extending his hands to the faerie.

"He was promoted!" Syn'ella's excitement turned to dread when she saw the knight offer her a crumpled patch. The patch was the symbol on all knights' cloaks, denoting the symbol of Branthian; this one was stained with a tiny drop of blood. "No..."

"Knight-Captain Feskar said to give this... to the bravest warrior he had ever faced in battle," the knight bowed reverently and dropped to one knee. "Your grief is ours, Brave Syn'ella."

"How?" Silver tears fell once more as she held the patch. She had wounded him in battle to get his help, and they had become comrades in arms after that. He became her friend.

"The dead coming out of the wastes, led by a dark knight. His stand allowed us to get the villagers here ahead of the horde."

The faerie clenched her tiny fists but kept her anger to herself. Releasing it in a sigh, she lifted his face and looked at him. “I will treasure this as long as I can draw my blade,” Syn’ella said with honor as her tears fell.

“Look!” Gallus cried as he stood up and looked out at where the storm had been.

Syn’ella wiped away tears and flew over, seeing what was still coming. An army of the dead still approached the city, a massive swath of shambling figures. With a dark army on one side and a force of the dead on the other, they were still in for the fight of their lives.

Ruins of the Lonely Tower, Endless Wastes

He felt his spell collapse and screamed in fury, sending a stack of ancient books scattering across the dusty floor with a wave of his hand. “How?! The elves don’t have the power to do this, and the Branthian sorcerers wouldn’t even know what to do.” Raer’dreth was tired and losing what little patience he even had. The war had just started, and already his knights were being killed faster than he could safely bring them back. He was burning through his power quickly; if this kept up, he would soon be exhausted. Luckily, he was an archmage and, as such, his reserves of power were deep. Still….

“They are working together against you, Spawn of Darkness,” Alant said in the calm tone that had been eating at Raer’dreth ever since his bloodmages had brought the young boy and Samor here.

Raer'dreth had bound the young man in manacles forged by the ancient Jal'riens and chained him to the wall. Those manacles were said to block magic from finding the person bound; his friends wouldn't be coming to save him. As for Samor—the dark knight turned abomination—it was even easier. Once Samor Cah was within Raer'dreth's sight, the dark elven archmage strengthened the spell he used to control his dark knights, and Samor Cah stopped fighting his restraints. Samor was fully back under his control—all but his mouth, apparently.

"Look at that, *Master,*" the dark knight said with a mocking tone from his corner. He leaned against the wall, watching Alant with his empty skull and glowing green eyes. "This young whelp knows more than you do." The Knight of Shad'ar screamed as violet lightning arced into him from Raer'dreth's hands.

"I said to keep quiet, abomination. You may think that my spells might not have much effect on your new form, but I haven't really tried yet." Raer'dreth turned his attention back to his table, fuming at the resilience of the elves and humans. He had sent Samor to the elven nation of Tsir'illia first to weaken them and prevent this very thing from happening, but then this young whelp got involved, and everything spiraled out of his control since then. *So, what makes this young one so special?* he asked himself as he started to calm down.

The dark elven archmage looked over at the sword the bloodmage had taken from the child and shook his head. Raer'dreth had known of that sword back when he destroyed the lands he was standing on. Ilen'dar, the sword of Light, and its twin, Dar'kir, were famous swords of twin Jal'rien heroes. He couldn't even recall their names now.

"It all comes back to you, doesn't it, Alant?" Raer'dreth asked as he walked over to the boy. "You stopped Samor from destroying the faeries, then warned the elves," the dark elf said, as he paced around his workroom. "They gave you this sword, and then you killed my Knight of Shad'ar with it. Who are you, really?"

"I think the time is finally upon you to know that, dark spawn," Alant said in a deeper tone.

"Go on..." Raer'dreth had thought he was one step ahead of everyone all this time, but lately, he suspected a higher power thwarted him at every turn.

"I am the reincarnation of Gar'heth—God of Honor and Battle," Alant said majestically.

"So, a God sent his mortal to stop me?" Raer'dreth asked with a raised brow.

The boy relaxed and smiled, "No, you're just gullible."

"*Fool!*" Raer'dreth sent an arc of violet lightning into the boy; Alant screamed and thrashed in his manacles, his muscles bulging as he fought the pain. "Who do you think you are dealing with?" Raer'dreth said, as he poured more and more into the boy, watching him writhe on the sandy floor, blood leaking from his ears now.

"He knows who he is dealing with, *Master*. That is why he is trying to get you to kill him," Samor said from his corner.

Raer'dreth stopped and took a calming breath, reigning in his anger. He wouldn't give Samor the satisfaction of acknowledgment. Another soul gem glowed as a Knight of Shad'ar was slain. The dark elven archmage sighed and walked over to bring the knight back. He worked the spell, and the soul rose out of the gem, then sank into the floor, off to find a new body on the field of battle. *What else could go wrong today?* he asked himself. A lot of the soul gems were shattered as Samor's had been, but he still had enough to deal with these fools. He never saw the knowing look that Alant and Samor shared, nor did he notice that the Sword of Light wasn't where he had placed it.

City Gates of Branth, Nation of Branthian

She grinned as her axe slammed into the dead and blasted the rib cage away. It didn't slow the damned thing at all, but it made her feel good. Falgrim was starting to get tired—hells, they all were. The sun had finally risen and greeted them with yet more battle. Rather than wait for the forces to pin them in, the heroes rallied the remaining knights, dwarves, and anyone else who could fight and pushed the dark warriors towards the gates of the city instead of the docks. Here, they joined the approaching dead, but at least they were all in front of them.

"Another one is back," Anatarn said as a body stood wreathed in smoking armor. The tall warrior swung Dar'kir in wide arcs, taking out the howling warriors from Raer'drin and the dead. The enchanted sword slicing through bone and armor effortlessly. Ever since it had been near Ilen'dar, the sword had gained power somehow. He held up the shield on his arm, blocked another attack, and smiled at Falgrim.

Falgrim hurled her axe at the shadowknight and took off its arm before the thing could fully solidify. "And stay down!" she swore as she rolled out of the way of an axe and grabbed her own. She spun to block the next attack, just as the man howled and clutched his back. Falgrim took the opening and slashed the man's throat, just as Syn'ella pulled her sword out of the man's spine.

"Nice work, Falgrim," the faerie warrior said before she flew off. She never believed it when she first heard it, but

Falgrim had to admit that the Warrior of the Ninth Thorn was a tiny force to be reckoned with. "So, you're not mad?" she called out to Anatarn.

"No, Love. I get why you didn't say anything. But we're talking about this bond when this is all over," Anatarn called back, raising the Banner of Branthian for all to see. "Forward!" The silver shield had become like a standard for the fighters of Branthian, the actions of the tall warrior inspiring the knights and dwarves alike.

Falgrim waded into the horde and kicked and slashed, catching up with Belsa and Grym to save Knight-Commander Lawson and his small group. The three dwarves stood back-to-back as the dead came, and fought methodically, taking legs then heads, clearing space around them so the knights could finish them on the ground with spears. She looked up and found her love in the distance, his height making him stand out among the hunched dead and smaller holy warriors. Her heart swelled with both love and pride, and it was right there that Falgrim realized that she had accepted the heartbond. *How did this ever happen to me?* she thought as she smiled, hacking away at another dead warrior with a curved sword.

An explosion rocked the center of the dead, bodies flying as the fire grew outward. Bones clattered on the ground like rain as Eliyan stood by the gate and wove her arms again, sending another ball of liquid fire into the enemy.

"That's me, girl!" Falgrim cheered as the dwarven axe-for-hire fought more of the dead around her. They almost had this side clear enough to break away and leave the rest to the knights. She had started this little adventure hating magic, yet now she had grown to see its usefulness.

"That's a good sign," Belsa said, her chest heaving with exhaustion. "That must mean the bloodmages are all gone."

"I don't think they're gone, but more likely the rest fled when the tide of battle turned," Grym said, as his axe bounced off the skull of a dead warrior. Knight-Commander Lawson promptly skewered the leg of the dead and dropped it, allowing Grym a second chance to smash it.

Falgrim was going to say something witty and sarcastic, but her gut wrenched with an unknown fear. In a panic, she sought out Anatarn and found him. "No!" Falgrim cried out, dashing through the dead like a battering ram. Anatarn was standing alone against Callen Drah.

He can't...not by himself, she thought as she frantically fought to get to her Love. *Wait for me, Anatarn...just fall back and wait.* Yet, in her heart, she knew he wouldn't. Rolling through a small crowd of barbaric warriors, she saw Callen dance around Anatarn, both of them trading blows and sending sparks into the air. The dwarf ran and fought, screaming his name over and over. Then she heard him.

Over the din of battle, Anatarn was singing. It was that dippy song they had danced to in Llar; tears sprang to her eyes as she fought to get to him. *No, no, no, don't ye give up on me, An!* Falgrim's mind raced as she wrestled through the horde, but she kept getting caught and having to fight her way through. "Syn'ella!" Falgrim called out as tears fell, her sobs choking her. "Get to him, *please*!"

"On the way!" Syn'ella called back, flying up out of the throng and heading toward Anatarn. The tiny faerie was covered in blood, and her wings were torn here and there, but she still kept herself aloft. Just when hope started to form in Falgrim's mind, Syn'ella was thrown back by a club, the large weapon swinging up like an avalanche. Syn'ella tried to get her slim sword in line to block, but the massive weapon swatted her away like she was nothing. She didn't get back up.

Falgrim punched and kicked, swinging her axe like a madwoman, as she clawed her way to Anatarn. Just as she broke through, she saw them fighting—thrust, parry, shield, parry. Then suddenly they both lunged at once, Dar'kir slamming into Callen's heart and bursting out of her back.

Please, please, please, she cried in her mind as Anatarn's shield arm dropped. Time seemed to stand still as Falgrim kept running, shouldering the straggling dead out of her way as her heavy boots thundered on. Anatarn turned to her, Callen's sword of ash buried in his chest. Anatarn smiled at her one last time and fell to his knees, already burning away from the ash pouring into him; his eyes never left hers.

"Noooooo!" Falgrim screamed in agony, her wail of despair giving even the dead pause for a second. The dwarven warrior fell to her knees, wailing into the ground as tears streamed down her cheeks, her rage and loss burning inside of her chest like a consuming wave of fire. She scrambled over to where Anatarn was and grabbed Dar'kir from the pile of warm ash, screaming her anger to the heavens. With her axe, R'dar, in one hand and the dark sword in her other, she leapt up and tore through *anyone* who stood against her. *"All of you will die!"*

"Falgrim! Wait!" Syn'ella called after her, the faerie's whole left side bruised and her left eye swollen. The faerie warrior flew beside the dwarf and tried to get her to stop, but she was ignored.

Falgrim wasn't even defending herself anymore. She launched herself into groups of the dead and just cut them down while screaming her grief, letting blows land on her back, sides, and arms as she cut the dead down relentlessly. The human combatants fled rather than face her and were cut down by the knights rallying behind the horrible force of nature that was Falgrim's grief. Even the remaining Shadowknights didn't fare well, as her tactics weren't skill but pure rage and fury; she didn't care about herself.

"For Falgrim! For Anatarn!" the knights and dwarves cried as they cleared the field behind the enraged dwarf. Not one knight dared get too close to the seemingly berserk warrior; only Syn'ella dared keep up with her—she and another dwarf.

"Fal! Fal, you have to stop!" Belsa cried out, as she charged behind the grief-stricken dwarf carrying the silver shield now, "Don't give in like this, *please!"*

Falgrim wasn't sure why this plea got through to her, and the others didn't, but she stopped as she slammed her axe into an undead skull, shattering it into pieces. *"Give in?!"* she cried, her voice now hoarse. "I haven't given in, Belsa. I'm going to make them all *pay!*"

"Falgrim, look at yourself. You're bleeding from over a dozen wounds and taking so many hits that your armor is all but useless. I don't want to lose you, too," Belsa pleaded, as she carefully approached the dwarven woman.

Falgrim screamed again, even louder than before, and sank to her knees. "He's *gone*, Belsa...I can't *feel* him!" Falgrim slammed the ground over and over as the Knights of the Realm rode past, cleaning up the dead still coming.

"Oh, Falgrim.... Sweet Gar'heth...you were heartbonded," Belsa said, falling to her knees beside her friend, her own tears now falling into the dirt.

"If I die in battle, then I can see him...I just..." Whatever Falgrim was going to say was lost as she choked, hearing a familiar voice come from behind her.

"I don't want you to die, Love."

Falgrim spun, swinging Dar'kir in an arc and hitting only air as the spirit of Anatarn stood before her. He was transparent and fading fast; yet, it was him, right down to his ridiculous wide-brimmed hat. The dwarf surged forward and tried to grab him, and hit the dirt hard, her tears mixing with blood. "You were supposed to wait for me...You weren't supposed to *leave ME!*" she wailed, collapsing into a sobbing ball on the ground.

"I know. I couldn't let Callen go. She was trying to get away, and I saw my chance," the spirit of Anatarn said. His voice was getting quieter now as he bent down. "I have to go, but I needed to give you something first, Dear." The spirit held out both hands and pushed them into Falgrim's shoulders as if trying to hug her, smiling.

"You're giving her a part of you, aren't you?" Syn'ella asked.

"Yes. Kysen's spirit told me how you did this with her, Syn'ella. You gave me a way to save her from her grief," Anatarn said, as he faded even more. "Promise me, Falgrim."

"Promise ye what?" she asked in a small voice, sitting up as she continued to cry. The pain was less now, though, yet she knew it would never truly fade.

"Promise to carry the sword and remember me...." The spirit vanished then, and the silence on the field was palpable.

"Everyone else saw that, too, right?" Syn'ella asked, breaking the quiet.

"Yes, though I don't believe it," Belsa said, as she stood slowly. "Look, the fallen aren't getting up anymore."

"Raer'dreth's spell fades, finally. Something must be taxing the dark elf," Eliyan said, as she came running to them amidst the carnage.

Falgrim stood with Dar'kir and R'dar and hung her head. She saw some of the dark knights starting to rise once more and grinned. *I promised ye, but I don't have to like it,* she thought. "Eliyan, you better get to work on me. My new sword and I still have work to do."

Ruins of the Lonely Tower, Endless Wastes

He tried again for the hundredth time to break the manacles, to no avail. He knew he couldn't possibly snap the enchanted metal, but he had to try something. Alant Landsir had been in chains since he was dragged here by the bloodmages, bound in these manacles, and thrown in the corner. He had slept off and on, not quite sure how long he had been here at this point. The young Silverlord looked over at Samor Cah—no longer just a Shadowknight, but an abomination with only a skull for a head and glowing green eyes—and frowned. The creature was an enigma that had Alant rethinking his hatred toward the malicious dark knight. After all, they had both been working together to keep the dark elf wizard off balance with their words. *Not as much after that round of violet lightning*, he thought. *That really hurt.*

Alant thought about all the times Samor Cah had the opportunity to kill him and never took it. The dark knight's excuse was that it was dishonorable, and that sent Alant's mind reeling. The young Silverlord could not possibly imagine what kind of twisted code of honor let someone slaughter innocent people. Somehow, though, it bound Samor Cah to his word

Alant recalled Samor even saying as much to Lord Knight Joran the first time Alant had laid eyes on the dark knight. Samor had said: *Yet, I am compelled to give fair warning to an honorable foe. Prophecy tinged with dark magic surrounds my fate, and, as such, no Knight can ever hope to wound me in battle*. Then, later, he mentioned it again. *Honor...the one thing that can compel me still.*

Now, Alant and Samor were working together to keep Raer'dreth distracted as much as they could. Alant had noticed that after making Raer'dreth hit him over and over with magic, the hold on Samor had weakened again. Raer'dreth had commanded him not to move, but for the last few hours, Samor could move without Raer'dreth noticing. He had taken Ilen'dar from where Raer'dreth had kept it, slowly maneuvering it near Alant. not that he could do anything in these manacles, though.

"Curse them all to the deep hells!" Raer'dreth swore as another crystal went dark. This one seemed special, standing out from the rest.

"Looks like Callen Drah finally met her match," Samor said with that sly tone. "I would've given anything to see that. She was one hell of a fighter."

Alant frowned again, hearing genuine praise from the abomination standing in the corner. "Was she your...friend?" Alant asked. He was beyond curious now, and he had nothing else to do.

"Friend? Not quite. We were knights together a very long time ago. Not unlike yourself, actually," Samor said, as Raer'dreth started casting his spell of summoning once more. "We were Dragonknights of Jal'rien and lived by a strict code of battle." Samor's tone quieted and became almost morose as he talked.

"I didn't know," Alant confessed. He was going to ask more, but Raer'dreth slumped against his work table, his hand in mid-air. In front of him was a ball of translucent energy—the soul of a dark knight. It was supposed to fly down into the ground now, but sat in the air, quivering.

"Why do you fight me?" Raer'dreth asked with barely constrained rage.

"Because you're too weak to force me any longer, master," the voice of Callen Drah said as the ball formed into her likeness. She resembled a spirit more now and stood defiant. "I have done terrible things in your name, and I am tired of it. We followed you blindly all those centuries ago, not knowing the depth of your evil. Now, thanks to one valiant warrior, this is the day I find my freedom." Callen threw up her arms and, in a flash of light, transformed. Gone was the armor of the dark knights, and in its place was a beautiful young woman with flowing copper hair in an ancient uniform. "You have no hold on me any longer, Raer'dreth." Callen floated past the enraged archmage as he tried spell after spell to contain her. She briefly nodded at Samor before turning towards Alant.

"I am sorry, young Silverlord. Your friend, Anatarn, fought well and with honor. In the end, he struck a killing blow with his blade, Dar'kir, knowing it would leave him open to my blade as well. I will honor his courage in the afterworld." With that, she floated up and dissipated in a shower of light.

Alant looked up just in time to see Raer'dreth—face consumed with rage—flick his hands out as his fingers twisted. A searing pain shot through Alant as shadows spiraled up from the floor, twisting around his legs. It felt like the shadows were biting him, a hundred little mouths feeding on his flesh. "You won't...break...*me!*" Alant cried out, clawing at his legs futilely.

"There is the great elven archmage I've come to know," Samor said as he stood tall now, his green eyes flaring brightly in his bare skull. "Attacking a helpless whelp in chains..."

"You!" Raer'dreth screamed, finally having had enough of the monstrous knight. He crooked his fingers once more and lashed out with the violet lightning. The energy slammed into Samor and brought him to his knees as the dark knight screamed, his jaw stretching impossibly wide in his bare skull.

Alant tried to breathe as the shadows writhing on his legs faded. With the archmage's focus switching to Samor, the magic lessened. *He is weakening... If only I could get free*, Alant swore to himself as he flexed his arms once again. He kicked and twisted as Samor writhed on the ground. Then, Raer'dreth gasped out loud as the dark knight started to stand.

"Yes, *master*, your spells do cause me agony, but they also serve a purpose," Samor said, struggling to his feet. His eerie voice never even sounded like he was in pain, mainly because he had no air in his dead lungs. "They serve to weaken you enough so I may gain my freedom!" Samor stood triumphantly, snatching Ilen'dar from its hiding place near Alant, and swung the blade down as hard as his preternatural strength would let him. The blade sheared through the chains holding Alant and gave him freedom at last.

"Fools! Do you think you stand against a powerful sorcerer or an elven wizard?" Raer'dreth spat as he wove his hands in a circle. "I am Raer'dreth Iliad, of House Iliad, and I am *the* dark elven archmage!" Dozens of shadow tendrils leapt from his fingers, arcing towards both Samor and Alant.

Alant stepped in front of Samor and took them all on his blade, sweeping it in an arc from left to right and dissipating the shadows with a flare of light from Ilen'dar. "He talks as much as you do, Samor," Alant said, as he assumed a wide stance. *He isn't wrong, though.* Alant thought as they all circled each other. *Tired or not, Raer'dreth is still an archmage, with legendary reserves and power according to the stories.* He dodged a bolt of violet lightning and rolled, gaining his feet in time to take a ray of flame on the blade and fall to a knee from the impact of it.

Samor blasted out at Raer'dreth with his eyes, the sickly green ray blasting the work table as Raer'dreth ducked behind it. The archmage spun his fingers in a pattern and shot the crumbling debris right back at the dark knight. The pieces of the stone table slammed into the former Knight of Shad'ar one at a time, relentlessly driving him into the wall as the entire room shook.

As dust rained down from the ceiling, Alant rushed the dark elf and swung Ilen'dar in a slashing pattern; once, twice, three times Raer'dreth blocked the blade with bursts of shadow, but the last one got through, clipping the archmage on the shoulder and cutting deep.

"Away, whelp!" Raer'dreth screamed in pain and shock, blasting Alant with azure fire that washed over the sword and ate at the youth.

Alant fell screaming, the pain eating at his very nerves was unbearable. He tried to put out the flames, but they wouldn't stop; he kept burning. *Wait...my clothes*, he thought through the pain. *They're not burning*. Alant tried to focus his thoughts away from the pain and struggled to rise. As he did, the flames went away, taking the pain with them. It had been an illusion. "Nice try, wizard..." Alant said through gritted teeth, as he stood fully. Only to be blasted in the chest by a small ball of actual fire. Alant hit the back wall hard, his clothes and skin charring black as he screamed in agony for real this time. The fire ate at his skin as he writhed on the ground.

Samor finally pushed the stone blocks away and crawled out, firing his eyes again at Raer'dreth with a yell of defiance. "Die!" The green rays shot out but were caught in a net of shadow. Raer'dreth was ready this time.

Raer'dreth smiled tiredly and flung the ball of green light back at Samor. The explosion hit the dark knight in the chest, rocking the underground chamber, making the entire structure shake even more. Larger debris fell now, as the dark elf stood tall. "You two had no chance to prevail against me, but I will give you both a nod for the effort," he began as he leaned against a pillar, clearly near exhaustion. The dark elf pushed off and limped towards Samor, cracking his wrists. "Now, let us see how much it will take to end you for good, shall we?"

"You talk too much," Alant said weakly as Raer'dreth turned, just in time to see Ilen'dar slam into his chest. Raer'dreth choked as a brilliant light burst out of his back, spraying the archmage's blood everywhere. Raer'dreth cried out in shock and pain, grasping the stained blade as it glowed, nearly severing his fingers. The dark elf dropped to his knees, gasping.

Alant collapsed with him as he pulled his sword free. "That was for…my friends." The Silverlord slumped back, fighting to stay conscious amid the pain, pushing himself up to his elbow.

Raer'dreth tried to send healing energy into his chest from his damaged fingers, but Samor pounced on him, wrestling his arms out wide and head-butting the dark elf to keep him prone.

"Flee, Alant. I will finish this," Samor said, as he held the archmage down. Raer'dreth blasted the dark knight with spells, but his power was fading quickly.

"No, we can..." Alant started, but he could barely sit up, let alone fight anymore. He clutched the charred wound in his chest and knew it was bad. His whole body shook, and he was cold. He tried once more, finally gaining his feet as the two combatants rolled and fought each other. Raer'dreth got free and spun his hands to open a portal...only to find it blocked by a green barrier.

Samor slammed his armored knee into Raer'dreth's ribcage, shattering that whole side and pinning the archmage down once more as he looked up at Alant. His skull was cracked now, green light leaking from most of the joints in his armor. "I want you to know, Alant, that I was wrong. I traded my life for dishonor, and now I follow Callen Drah; yet, I will take this one with me." Samor Cah laughed as Raer'dreth screamed in frustration, his blood mixing with the stone dust. "Now, go and live with honor, Silverlord."

Alant nodded with solemn eyes, saluting the fallen knight. He stumbled out of the room with Ilen'dar and crawled up a sand-filled ramp, looking back as Samor looked up and shot green flames out of his eyes and mouth, blasting the already weakened ceiling and bringing the whole thing down. Alant Landsir crawled a few more feet, seeing the blue sky and dozens of souls drifting high into the sky. He collapsed, his vision fading to black. He never noticed the enchanted manacles fall off his wrists as the temple collapsed inwardly.

EPILOGUE — JUST GETTING STARTED

Inner Courtyard, Castle Branth

She limped down the stone stairs, helping the queen take one step at a time. Hylana was alive, but barely. The massive ritual spell that the collective wizards and sorcerers pulled off drained life force from all of them, some more than others. Some bodies turned to dust before their eyes, while others were just...empty husks. They all knew this could happen going into it, and Hylana fully expected to fade away at the climax of the spell. *Yet again, another person sacrificed themselves instead of me*, she thought bitterly. The elven wizard Kysen had even taken Tolandra's burden, wanting to power the spell with her own life so she could be with her beloved, Ereval, in the afterlife. *The Forever Lands, I think Ereval called it.*

The battle was over, the dead collapsing, and the dark knights no longer getting back up. The rest of the barbaric warriors had retreated to their ships, sailing south, and the forces of Branthian mourned their dead. Yet, no sign of Alant had been seen. A trumpet sounded from the king's chambers, and King Danrae came out with Alsan Brenshin of Lorant and two knights flanking them. Healed as he was, the dark wound had taken a lot out of the king, but he was already on his feet.

Before anyone could say anything, the outer courtyard gate opened as Syn'ella came flying in, her face bruised and her left side a bloody mess. Falgrim came walking behind, the dwarf still holding Dar'kir in a death grip, her axe lost in the battle. Her wounds were bandaged, yet her eyes seemed haunted. Behind Falgrim came Belsa—looking rough with a gaping wound on her leg and her right arm in a sling—and the dwarf with the flamboyant hat, limping from an arrow still in his thigh.

"Anatarn?" Alsan asked as she let the king stand on his own now and searched for signs of the tall warrior in black. Her only answer was Falgrim finally crumpling to the ground, her sobs wracking her stout form, the dark sword clattering to the dirt.

"He took out Callen..." Belsa said sadly, leaving his fate hanging in the air.

"I feel him!" Syn'ella said in shock as she fluttered down to the dirt, holding her chest as if hurt.

"Alant?" Tolandra asked with a note of hope in her lyrical voice.

"Yes. I knew he was somewhere to the north, but I couldn't pinpoint it. Now, though, I can tell exactly where he is." Silver tears fell as she stood, her whole body shaking with sobs. "He's so hurt, My Queen...we have to get to him...he's so cold!"

"Syn'ella, Warrior of Tsir'illia. I don't have anything left to open a portal. We...it took everything to stop that storm..." The queen couldn't look at Syn'ella as she delivered the tragic news.

"I'm exhausted, too, Syn'ella," Eliyan said, as she came in behind them. The young elven healer looked ragged and pale, her eyes sunken and her arms listless as she dropped next to

Falgrim, wrapping the dwarf in her arms. It looked like she had healed everyone on the battlefield and was a walking corpse. She shared a look with the Queen of Lorant, and Alsan nodded.

"There must be something someone can do?" King Danrae asked as they all came together under the rising sun. "It can't be a coincidence that the dead fell and the dark forces fled right when this brave warrior can finally sense Alant. He must've saved us all."

Hylana smiled. This is what she was here for. This was her redemption. "Syn'ella, where is he?" the High Sorceress asked, standing tall.

Syn'ella closed her eyes and scrunched up her bruised face, wiping away her tears. "In the middle of the Endless Wastes." The tiny faerie gasped, clutching her chest. "I can feel him...he is fading quickly. Oh, my Love! I can feel him slipping!"

Hylana limped over and laid a hand on the faerie, tapping into her heartbeat. She had seen both Ereval and Kysen do this…giving everything to the magic, fueling it with their own life. She wasn't sure how, but she would be damned if she failed them now. That young boy came into her life and saved her, now it was her turn. Hylana clutched her gemstone around her neck, the amethyst cracked from all the fighting. The gem would work, but not much longer. "Farin," she whispered, and almost instantly she could see where Syn'ella could feel, using the faerie's senses as a guide to the fallen hero. Hylana's chest hurt, but she was determined not to let anyone else die for her. *Not one more...*

"What is it with you, Branthians and Tsir'illians rushing towards your death?" a husky voice said from behind Hylana. Hylana turned to see Alsan Brenshin holding the High Sorceress's shoulder. Warm energy flooded into the sorceress as the Queen of Lorant smiled. "Let's go get your hero."

"But you're not..."

"Let's worry about what I may or may not be, later."

Hylana concentrated on the feeling from Syn'ella, then saw a figure in the sand by some buried ruins. "Portan," she whispered as she gave her life force to the spell. Instead of consuming her, the magic was also fueled by Alsan's magic using Hylana as a conduit. The portal snapped open, and since Hylana and Alsan were connected through the spell, it sent all three to the sandy location.

Alant came awake to the sound of chimes clinking in a light breeze, the scent of lilac and vanilla heavy in the air. Sitting up, he realized he was dressed in clothes that were not his own: shirt and breeches of the finest white silk. "Where am I?" he asked aloud, looking around the room he found himself in. The windows were curtained with satin drapes, and gemstones lined the walls in strange patterns. Even the floor was intricately etched with beautiful scenes of flowers and trees.

I've been here before, he thought as the scene played out before him.

"You're not in Dyln'ir, good knight," a soft voice said, the tone seeming playful, yet cautious.

Alant ran his fingers over his chest, expecting the vicious wound to flare with pain, yet his skin was whole and unmarred under his shirt.

No, this isn't right. This is a memory. That wound was different than the one Raer'dreth gave me.

Alant looked towards the voice and saw—not a woman as he had in his memory, but Ereval sitting on the floor cross-legged.

"Ereval?" Alant asked, standing and walking over urgently. "What is going on?"

"You're visiting in the Forever Lands, dear Silverlord," the elven archmage said. The elf was dressed in flowing white robes with his long white hair tied in a ponytail. He walked to the window and waved, inviting Alant.

Alant could sense an inner peace to the entire room—no, the very air. "What are the Forever Lands?" he asked warily, although Alant had a really good guess that he didn't survive the fight with the dark elf after all.

"I can see that you've already guessed it, but fear not, brave Silverlord. I said you were visiting." Ereval walked over and hugged him. "I need you to deliver a message for me," the elf said.

Come back to me...

The words were distant and echoed around the room. Alant couldn't see anyone but felt that he should know who it was. A tug, deep in his chest, that made his heart sing.

"Ah, you don't have long, Alant. They found you." Ereval smiled and pressed a stone into Alant's hands, folding his fingers over it. "Give this to Hylana for me."

Please Alant...Come back, my Love!

Alant came to, coughing sand and blood, the warm wind whipping sand everywhere and blinding him. Tiny arms squeezed his throat hard, and kisses rained down upon his cheek and eyes.

"Yes. Yes, yes, yes! You're alive," Syn'ella cried, her silver tears falling all over Alant's neck. "Thank Amara, Alant, you're alive. My Love!"

Alant opened his eyes to see Alsan and Hylana staring at him with exhausted looks on their faces. "What are you two doing here?" he asked, a bit bewildered at it all. He looked back at the temple and saw the ruins, shaking his head. "He saved us all."

"Who did, Alant? We assumed you saved us?" Hylana asked, sinking to her knees.

"Samor Cah. We fought Raer'dreth, and he pinned him down and blasted the roof. It caved in on them both." The young Silverlord struggled to stand, using his sword as a crutch, as Syn'ella tugged with all her might. He looked at the faerie for the first time and saw the wounds covering her, his heart sinking. "Oh, gods, you're hurt."

"It's alright," she assured him, flying all around him. "I'll live. More importantly, so will you."

"Thank you for healing me, Hylana. I owe you again."

"It wasn't me, Alant." Hylana looked over at the Queen of Lorant and smiled weakly.

Alant cocked his head to the side and looked at Alsan, then remembered his dream. *Was it a dream, though?* Alant looked down at his hands, and there was a stone. The perfectly round gem was a polished and vibrant amethyst, complete with a tiny silver hook in it for a chain. "I think this is for you, Hylana," Alant said, handing over the gem.

"Where...how did you find this?" Hylana asked clearly, beside herself. "Did you get this inside the temple?"

"No. Ereval gave me this when I saw him in my dream. I was somewhere called..."

"The Forever Lands," Hylana answered for him, her tears falling as she clutched the gemstone to her chest. The stone flared with light, infusing the High Sorceress with a glow that seemed to heal her completely, body and soul. “Oh, Ereval,” she whispered as she flexed her arms. “I’m not even tired anymore.”

“Good. Now, let’s get home and rest. We can all talk about things once we're healed and rested,” Alsan said, as she nodded to Hylana. “I’ve got him, if you can take her?” Alsan grabbed Alant and wove her fingers, opening a portal to Branthian.

Castle Wrath, Isle of Raer’drin.

They both sat down at once as the image of the Lonely Tower showed it crumbling into a pile of rubble, the green glow of their spell fading. They were exhausted from keeping up the shield to prevent their father from escaping, keeping him there to meet his fate, a fate they made happen. Ril and Xil Iliad—the prophet twins—smiled at each other as the sun’s rays shone through the windows, lighting up the dark workroom; it was their workroom now.

“We did it, brother,” Ril said finally once his breathing was under control. He looked around and felt an emptiness pervading the castle. It was a welcome emptiness for sure, but it definitely was strange.

“Father will never be able to threaten us again,” Xil said, getting up slowly. “I still can’t believe we pulled it off, though. So much could’ve gone wrong.”

Ril laughed softly and nodded to his twin. “It was a gamble, but one that finally paid off after all these years.” When their father had tasked them to weave prophecy around the two Knights of Shad'ar, they each had a vision of how the Dark War would play out. That gave them chances to alter some of the things and eventually cause the downfall of the great archmage, Raer'dreth. Giving Samor and Callen the weakness of the two swords of legend, knowing that those swords would be in play at the final battle, was a stroke of genius.

"Do you still want to carry on like we planned? Pulling back a little bit and taking the lands around Oliar?" Xil asked as he walked over to the map of Alian'tir. Their father's plan was total conquest, but the twins had seen a better way.

"Yes, alert the remaining ships that the battle is lost, but the war is not over. Have them head to Oliar and take the city. With Lady Nara there, it should be easy," Ril said, as he pulled his heavy cotton robe off and took a black silk robe off a peg. The ceremonial black silk robes were laced with gold embroidery signifying high station and were usually only worn by Raer'dreth for two reasons: executions and announcements. Now, the brothers would wear them so people would know who was in charge. "Then, we can take the fort and secure the villages for slaves as we fortify the south under our control."

"Should I let the reserve ships know to set sail for Oliar as well?" Xil asked, as he, too, found a matching black silk robe, donning it with a smile.

"I will handle that personally, brother." This was the true gamble in their plan, but one that had succeeded far greater than they had ever hoped. Ril and Xil had gone down to cast spells on the seventeen great black ships and revealed their power to the people of Raer'drin almost two tendays ago now. The people had, predictably, started worshiping them as the children of the God Raer'dreth, and the twins had used that to their advantage. They commanded that five ships should wait for their divine signal and hold back from the main fight.

“Personally? I thought you were staying here at the castle while I stayed on the mainland?” Xil asked with a raised eyebrow.

Ril walked over and laid a comforting hand on his brother’s shoulder. “I’m only stopping on the ship briefly, then I have to go scavenge as many of the soulgems I can find in the rubble of the Lonely Tower.” They didn’t need many, maybe four or so, to make captains in their new army. “After all, we need more undying warriors now that most of the dark knights have all been freed.”

“At least we still have two knights left for our generals,” Xil said as they walked over to the stone slabs. They had brought their father the soulgems, but had kept two here deliberately.

Ril patted the two glowing soulgems affectionately. “Now we have to keep them under our control, though.”

They both turned as one and held hands, their power growing exponentially as they twisted their fingers in concert. They had found that if they linked their power together, they were even more powerful than their father. They had used this to secretly give Samor Cah his powers and keep their father from controlling the abomination. “Then we can plan our next steps as Branthian realizes that they have lost the south.” The twins nodded in unison, both breaking into wide smiles as they walked out of their new workroom together. The great archmage Raer’dreth may have been thrown down, but the Dark War had only begun.

THE END, FOR NOW

APPENDIX

Albron Brenshin: King of Lorant and son of Alban Brenshin. Signed the treaty with the dwarves upon his father's death. Executed for crimes against the people.
Alant Landsir: Silverlord of Branthian and former squire of Lord Knight Joran. He is well over six feet tall with black hair and cinnamon eyes. Soulbonded to Syn'ella and wields the sword Ilen'dar, or Light as it's called in common.
Alsan Brenshin: The bastard daughter of the late Alban Brenshin and a half-elf sorceress. She is a little over five feet tall and thin, with long brown twin braids and deep brown eyes. Proclaimed Queen of Lorant after the execution of her brother Albron.
Anatarn Blackblade: Human warrior from Parsil in the south of Lorant. He has long black hair, dark eyes, and dresses in black leather armor with a wide-brimmed hat. Wields the sword Dar'kir or Dark as it's known in common. Heratbonded to Falgrim Ironhaft. Fell in the Battle of Branth.
Amara: Goddess of Nature and Magic. Revered by the elves and faeries, this goddess is worshipped by anyone who casts magic and lives in nature.

Ari'kel Everblade: Captain of the Queen's watch in Tsir'illia and accomplished wizard. She has long white hair and violet eyes. Dressed in white leathers and a flowing white cloak. Her tenacity is legendary, and she fights well with both sword and magic.

Balo Ferin: Sorcerer of Branthian with a small garnet stone and red robes.

Belsa Harlow: Female dwarf and Commander of the standing militia in Llar. Has dirty blond hair and blue eyes.

Bloodmage: Human sorcerers who have taken a darker turn. They use stones and words as well, but use blood as a catalyst to allow their spells to bypass wards and even armor, as it targets the very lifeblood of the enemy directly.

Branth: Capital city of Branthian and home to King Danrae's court. Fortified port city south of the King's Wood.

Branthian: Nation on the western coast of Alian'tir. Ruled by a democratic monarchy and protected by Knights of the Realm. Its capital is the fortified city of Branth.

Brenshin War: War between the dwarves of Xarvan Tor and Lorant over the rights of shard mining. A bloody conflict that saw the fall of King Alban Brenshin and started dwarven racism in Lorant.

Callen Drah: Female Knight of Shad'ar and undead warrior of Raer'dreth. She has long copper hair and twin pools of liquid fire for eyes. Known also as a Shadowknight from myth. Finally slain by Anatarn Blackblade.

Casius Coran: Knight-Captain of Oliar. He has piercing green eyes and long black hair, with a huge sword on his back.

Danni Hoarfren: Dwarven youth with brown hair and dark eyes. Three feet tall with the beginnings of a beard. Twin to Lanni Hoarfren, fell in the Forest of Dust.

Dravon: Retainer to Raer'dreth Iliad.

Dyln'ir: Capital city of Tsir'illia and home to the largest school for magic in all of Tsir'illia. Lies in the south of the Forest of Tsir.

Eldrian Danrae: King of Branthian. Lives in the capital city of Branth. He has grey hair and deep blue eyes. His crimson robes, trimmed with golden thread, display the silver crest of Branthian on his chest—a silver sun with a sword.

Eliyan Safril: Female elven wizard/healer from the house Safril in the city of Ulin'or. She has long white hair and deep violet eyes. Niece to Queen Tolandra of Tsir'illia

Endless Wastes: The wastes are a large section of parched desert in the center of Alian'tir. Created by foul magic during the ancient Wasting War between Branthian and Tsir'illia.

Eregon Noro: Lord of Oliar. He is a plump warrior with a decorative sword, killed by Belsa Harlow for revolting against his king.

Ereval Drial: Archmage of Dyln'ir. He has flowing white hair down his back and piercing violet eyes. Wears a white silk robe trimmed with gold and a cloak of diaphanous mesh. Soulbonded to Kysen Drial and an expert on history. Fell during the siege of Branth

Falgrim Ironhaft: Dwarven female axe for hire. From the dwarven mining city of Xarvan Tor in the Starsky mountains. Has thick hair done in three long, black braids hanging down her back. Short and well built. Heartbonded to Anatarn Blackblade.

Galbert Feskar: Knight-Captain of Fort Kaldrin in Branthian. Has black hair and grey eyes. Promoted after Knight General Marveth took over the Branthian Navy. Fell during the retreat of Fort Kaldrin.

Gallus Silverspear: Elven wizard from Tsir'illia with dark green robes. He has long white hair and burning green eyes. Owes a debt to Anatarn Blackblade.

Gar'heth: God of Honor and Battle. He is worshiped by warriors and knights, as well as most dwarves. He is often called upon before battle.
Gerick Eldon: High Sorcerer of Branthian, Fell during the siege of Branth.
Gnarr: Squat, filthy creatures with long matted hair and gray skin, covered in scars and warts. Their teeth are more often missing than not, and they have an appetite for just about anything.
Gravil Kar: Knight of Shad'ar with long blond hair spilling out from his helm.
Grinda Silversmith: Female dwarf who died during the Brenshin War. She was lost at the Stand of Brittleshan. Wife to Anatarn Blackblade.
Halin: Old man of Halstrad.
Haragrym Wordsplitter: Travelling merchant and writer of stories from Lorant. He is four feet tall, with a wide-brimmed hat trimmed with gold and a long mustache curled up at the ends. Has brown hair and dark eyes. Also known as Grym to his friends.
Hardin Lor: Knight of Shad'ar who killed the elven wizard wielding Dar'kir centuries ago.
Harvon: Village in the southern part of Lorant, overrun by the dead.
Heartbonded: See Soulbond
Hylana Brendal: Sorceress of Branthian. She has long black hair and green eyes. One of the most powerful sorcerers in Branthian due to her fast thinking and improvising. Promoted to High Sorceress after the death of Gerick.
Jaren Highleaf: High Wizard of Ulin'or and in charge of training the royal house Safril.

Jerix: God/Goddess of Thieves and Money. This god, perceived as both male and female at times, is worshipped by cutthroats and moneylenders as well as some dwarven miners.
Jimson Stoutfist: Male dwarven commander of the militia in Llar. He has brown hair, dark eyes, and a long brown beard, braided into three tails. Fell in the battle outside of Harvon.
Killen Everstone: Dwarven girl, short and stout, with long braided brown hair and deep grey eyes.
Kysen Drial: Lady of the capital city, Dyln'ir. She has long white hair entwined with violet flowers and deep amethyst eyes. Soulbonded to Ereval Drial and an accomplished wizard. Fell during the siege of Branth.
Lanni Hoarfren: Dwarven youth with brown hair and dark eyes. Three feet tall with peach fuzz for a beard. Twin to Danni Hoarfren.
Llor: Capital city of Lorant and seat of trade for the east coast. Home of the Brenshin court. A trade port city southeast of the Starsky Mountains. Ruled by Queen Alsan after her brother's execution.
Lorant: Nation on the eastern coast of Alian'tir. Ruled by a hereditary monarchy and protected by the Red Warriors of Lorant. Its capital is the trade city of Llor.
Lowen Weskel: Young sorceress from Branthian. She has short black hair and bright blue eyes. Studies primarily wind and wears a sapphire on a silver chain.
Malakath Hiram: Human sorcerer and blood mage in the northern town of Halstrad. Has pale skin, red hair, and his face is covered in freckles. Dresses in yellow and green and secretly works for Raer'dreth. Slain by Falgrim in Halstrad.
Marcus Joran: Lord Knight of the Realm in Branthian and expert in the Code of the Knight. He has short black hair that was graying on the sides and soft blue eyes. Slain by Samor Cah in Northern Branthian.

Millicent Whitetail: Lady in waiting to Tolandra Asil. Served the queen's mother before her and so on; thought to be ancient even by elven standards. Slain by Samor Cah in the storming of the Queen's tower, Tsir'ilia.
Nivia Nara: Consort to Lord Noro of Oliar. She is working with the twin prophets of Raer'drin to aid them in the Dark War.
Noral Percen: Knight of the Realm. He is stationed at Fort Kaldrin in Branthian.
Ongril Silvertree: Male elf and former steward to Eliyan Safril. He is from the city of Ulin'or in Tsir'illia. He has short white hair and emerald green eyes. Practiced in etiquette and the ways of most courts. Now advisor to Queen Alsan Brenshin of Lorant.
Oron Haves: Lieutenant of the Branthian guard based in Folris. He has close-cropped brown hair and dark eyes, along with a scar that runs down the entire right side of his face.
Raer'dreth Iliad: A dark elf of the great house Iliad and Ruler of Castle Wrath. He lives on the island of Raer'drin in Castle Wrath and has long white hair and grey eyes. Powerful archmage. Slain by Alant and Samor in the Lonely Tower.
Raer'drin: Island to the northwest of Alian'tir, populated by barbaric people who worship Raer'dreth as their god.
Reasen Dhal: Highmage to Archmage Raer'dreth, with long blond hair and piercing green eyes, wearing a large bloodstone around his neck. Bloodmage. Slain by Samor Cah.
Ril Iliad: Half-dark elf and prophetic wizard. He lives on the Isle of Raer'drin in Castle Wrath. He has faded white hair and ice blue eyes, and has an identical twin. Son to Raer'dreth
Samor Cah: Former Knight of Shad'ar and undead warrior. He was brought back in the rotting body of an ancient warrior and became an abomination. He has a bare skull for a face and twin pools of green fire for eyes.

Sarin Marveth: Knight General of the Knights of the Realm. Promoted to the leader of Branthian's navy. He has grey hair and brown eyes. Fell during the first battle at sea

Shadowknights: Creatures of myth and legend, these undead knights exist as souls that inhabit bodies that are recently slain. They rise and conform the body to their likeness and cannot be permanently slain by conventional weapons. Also known as Knights of Shad'ar.

Shar'in: Goddess of Death and Shadows. She is worshiped by murderers and malcontents as well as the Gnarr race, who call her Sar'in.

Shards: These tiny fragments of gold ore are mined by the dwarves for the rest of Lorant—the whole of Alian'tir, in fact. It is the standard currency of the continent.

Silver concordant: Centuries-old treaty between Tsir'illia and Branthian. A clause or addendum states the following: 'When the knight of shadows falls to the sword of a boy, the elves must give him their Light, and the humans their banner; only then can the Landsir rise and protect us all.'

Sorcerer: Humans who use special stones to focus magic and call upon their spells using forbidden words of power gained from dark entities.

Soulbond: Magical bonding between two people who are destined to be together for the rest of their lives. Rare among the races and extremely rare to cross races. Dwarves call it Heartbond.

Syn'ella: Faerie and holder of the Badge of the Ninth Thorn from Tsir'illia. She is only two and a half tall with gossamer wings, long golden hair, and golden eyes. Soulbonded to Alant Landsir.

Tenday: A Measure of time in the world of Alian'tir. It is exactly as it sounds, being the count of ten days' time.

Terran Lawson: Knight-Commander of Fort Kaldrin and Second in Command to Knight-Captain Feskar. Has blond hair and grey eyes.
The Code of the Knights: A Huge book, located in the capital city of Branth. It's thousands of pages detail everything a Knight of the Realm would need to act with both honor and courage in everyday life, hopefully, to aspire to Lord Knight someday.
Tolandra Asil: Half-faerie Queen of Tsir'illia. She lives in the isolated queen's tower in the north of Tsir'illia. Tolandra has long white hair, large gossamer wings, and deep sapphire eyes, and is a mix of elven and faerie descent.
Tsir'illia: Nation of elves and faeries in the north of Alian'tir. Ruled by an elected Queen or King and protected by elven wizards. It rests in the Forest of Tsir and all but its capital—Dyln'ir—is hidden from view.
Wizard: All wizards are either elven or half-elven and are trained in Tsir'illia. Wizards use hand gestures to command magic with grace and skill, and need no stones or words of power.
Xarvan Tor: Subterranean city of the dwarves in Lorant. Home of the dwarven war guild. Fortified city deep under the Starsky Mountains.
Xil Iliad: Half-dark elf and prophetic wizard. He lives on the Isle of Raer'drin in Castle Wrath. He has faded white hair and ice blue eyes, and has an identical twin. Son of Raer'dreth.
Yalen Dros: Youngest sorcerer in Branthian. He has blond hair and bright blue eyes, with a yellow stone to focus spells. Fell during the Siege of Branth
Zomnus: God of Luck and Fate. He is worshiped by almost everyone in Alian'tir in one way or another. He is often called upon before any big decision is made.

ABOUT THE AUTHOR

Born in the usual way, author **Michael D. Nadeau** found fantasy at the age of eight with Dungeons & Dragons. He loved being different people as well as casting magic. By High school he discovered his love for reading thanks to a teacher. She fed his thirst for books by bringing her own collections from home and lending them to him, even buying one towards the end of her class. He has now read hundreds of fantasy books, living in each of their worlds along with the characters. After a while, he started creating his own worlds for his games with friends. Cities, gods, ancient and terrible beings, and histories...then he would burn them all down.

He is the author of the Lythinall series: *The Darkness Returns* Book 1, *The Darkness Within* Book 2, *The Darkness Falls* Book 3, *Dragon Caller, Rise of the Archmage* Book 1, *Dragon Master; Rise of the Archmage* Book 2, *Tales from Lythinall*—an anthology, *The Curse of Seltemver: Tales of Lythinall* Book 2, and *Angels Among Us.* He also has several stories in Eerie River Publishing anthologies, as well as a few others.

For more of Daniel Eskridge's artwork, visit his website at:

https://daniel-eskridge.pixels.com/

www.ingramcontent.com/pod-product-compliance
Lightning Source LLC
Chambersburg PA
CBHW070225040826
49266CB00032B/471

* 9 7 8 1 9 6 0 6 5 4 0 6 9 *